WATCHING *for* *Mermaids*

DAVID H. ROPER

ISBN-10: 0615547648
ISBN-13: 9780615547640

Points East Publishing, Inc.
www.watchingformermaids.net
davidroper00@gmail.com

cover photo: the author aboard *Phyllis* — 1950s

PREFACE

The Truth.... Mainly

My two older brothers, my parents and I were all packed into the small dining room-turned bedroom in which my ailing, 82-year-old, bed-ridden mother had resided for over a year. We'd all been trying in vain to rouse her from a deep sleep.

"She's practicing being dead," my light-hearted oldest sibling said.

"No, she just doesn't want to listen to another one of David's sea stories," my middle brother jabbed.

"What did you say?" my nearly deaf father said.

"Dad, they're making fun of my sea stories, " I said toward him.

"What worries?" my ever-positive dad asked.

"STORIES. Making fun of my stories, not my WORRIES, Dad," I shouted.

Just then my mother moved in bed. We all stopped and looked at her. She opened her eyes. Then she said something. Very weakly. She was looking in my direction.

"She wants you, Dave. I think she wants to talk to you," my brother Skip said.

"HI MOM, WHAT IS IT?" I asked, leaning over her, inches from her face. "It's me, David."

"After 47 years I know what you look like," she said. Then she coughed in several short spasms. I adjusted the oxygen tube to her nostrils. After a few moments she caught her breath. "I've been listening, and I've been wondering," she said. "I've been wondering about these sea stories of yours. You know, David, if you actually *did* all the things you say you've done, the truth is you'd be twice my age by now."

"Mom, I don't make this stuff up... well, not all of it," I said. "And I like telling stories."

"Then why don't you write them all down and be done with it, so we can all get some rest," she said with a weak smile.

So, that's what I've done, Mom. And they're dedicated to you.

TABLE OF CONTENTS

I

CHILDHOOD

I

CHILDHOOD

There is a fifth dimension, beyond that which is known to man.
It is a dimension as vast as space and as timeless as infinity.
It is the middle ground between light and shadow,
between science and superstition.

For Reality, You See, Is Something Created by Man
To Dignify His Limitations

ROD SERLING

. . .

Since once I sat upon a promontory,
And heard a mermaid on a dolphin's back
Uttering such a dulcet and harmonious breath,
That the rude sea grew civil at her song,
And certain stars shot madly from their spheres
To hear the sea-maid's music.

WILLIAM SHAKESPEARE
A Midsummer Night's Dream

THE TRUTH ABOUT MERMAIDS

15 June, 1608 · Off the Artic Coast of Russia

In 1608, the English navigator Henry Hudson was skirting the polar ice off the arctic coast of Russia in his second attempt to find a northeast route to the spice markets of China. Near the coast of Nova Zembla, Hudson made his log entry of 15 June:

> *This morning, one of our companie looking over board saw a mermaid, and calling up some of the companie to see her, one more came up, and by that time shee was close to the ship's side, looking earnestly upon the men: a little after, a Sea came and overturned her: From the Navill upward, her backe and breasts were like a woman's.., her body as big as one of us; her skin very white; and long haire hanging down behinde, of colour blacke; in her going down they saw her tayle, which was like the tayle of a Porposse, and speckled like a Macrell.*

351 YEARS LATER

July, 1959 · 44.04N/68.35W
A small island just east of Isle au Haut, Maine

The Stem knows.

No one else until now, though.

Fifty one years ago, when I was nine years old, I saw two mermaids. Really. I understand why you might doubt me. So be it. But when I was nine years old I saw two mermaids. Period.

It could have been just another false sighting, another apparition, like the ones in those handwritten captains' logs of square-rigged vessels roaming the oceans looking for whales, or from the sailors' journals aboard the spice traders journeying back from Zanzibar. It could have been written off as just one more incident out of a young boy's imagination. But a stream of events flowed from that moment when I saw them, on that hot, languid day in July of the year 1959, that made me much different from other nine year olds. But more on that later.

Early on that morning of the sighting, my Dad and I had hidden from the heat under the canvas awning in the cockpit of *Phyllis*, our old wooden cutter. We were anchored in a rocky Maine cove which was somewhat open to the Northeast. Dad had hoped for a breeze to cool us, but it was not to be. The anchor line lay limp off the end of the bowsprit. The world seemed so still, I remember. Dad was working with a piece of manila anchor line in his lap. He held a small spool of heavy waxed thread between his knees, and was winding it around the end of the rope. On the end of the thread was a long, curved and rusty sewing needle. After he had wound about a half inch of thread around the line, he poked the needle through the middle of the line and pulled it tight. He did this several times. I watched him working so intently and with focus. I also watched a large drop of sweat run down the side of his face, hang for a moment at the end of his chin, and then drop onto his canvas pants. "What's that called, what you're doing?" I asked. "Whipping," he said. The word startled me, and I shifted on the canvas cockpit cushion, then leaned back, and looked away. "It's a sailor's term for tying off the end so it won't unravel. It's a way of caring for the life of the rope," he continued. "I'll teach you."

But I was suddenly nervous and wanted to get away by myself. "Maybe later Dad," I said.

"Why don't you get in the dinghy and practice your rowing?" he asked. I nodded. "Nice and calm now," he continued. "Good time for it. But don't forget your lifejacket...and please wear your hat."

The dinghy's bow line hung limp like the anchor line of the bigger boat. The totally calm and clear sea looked like a thick gel that held the reflections of the bow lines of the two boats in its midst like fruit in a jello. My sudden movement into the dinghy was startling in a world so still. I untied the bow line and pushed away from the big boat, picked up the wooden oars and slid them into their oar locks. The sudden shuffling of the oars echoed against the shore. "I might go ashore. Ok, Dad? Might do some beachcombing," I said.

I pulled toward shore, my eyes aimed down at my feet. The oars were adult oars, too long and heavy for me, and I had to concentrate. There was a small pool of water in the bottom of the boat, and I watched it move forward and aft with each motion of my oar strokes. I spread my feet to the side of the bilge, trying to keep them dry. Then I looked over my shoulder to check on my progress toward shore. The sandy beach and rocks and pine trees were getting close, and I began to smell the decaying seaweed left behind by the tide. The tide had been dead low and its flood was just now beginning. I knew that in its retreat six hours before it would have left other things behind. It would be a good time for beachcombing, I thought.

I walked perhaps a half mile, a long ways for a nine year old. Combing was good. I found three horseshoe crabs, those foot-long shelled creatures that look like miniature brown army tanks, their tails like great canons coming out of the turrets. I remembered, a couple of years earlier near my home in Massachusetts, when Sam

Cooper and I spotted our first horseshoe crabs. He had wanted to smash them with a big rock, either to kill them or see what was inside. Or maybe both. I remember trying to distract him as he lifted the rock, lying that I just spotted a deer in the high marsh grass, but Sam was intent on his goal. "Don't Sam," I said at the last second. He dropped the rock anyway, crushing the foot-long crab. Sam looked down at the gooey mess, then back at me. "Damn, you are such a wimp loser." Then he kicked over the crab and turned to look toward the tall marsh grass. "Now let's go find this wimpy deer of yours."

I moved on down the Maine beach, lost in my world of exploration. I found a bottle with a cork in it (though no note inside), a bright yellow orphaned lobster buoy, and a broken hockey stick. The bottle excited me the most because someday I knew I'd find one with a note in it. It might be a note from someone who was in trouble, and needed my help.

I was thinking about that, imagining where the note would be from, and how I would help, when I rounded a bend in the shore. I didn't realize it at first because I was looking down, but I was walking into a U shaped indentation made by years of hammering and then funneling of the Atlantic Ocean against the shore. It was a secluded nook, about thirty yards deep and fifty yards wide, and framed by two high, narrow arms of protruding rock. The nook's only access was at low tide, around these jutting walls, and along a short, normally submerged stretch of beach. The only other access was by boat, and I could see numerous nasty ledges now uncovered to seaward.

A gull flew close overhead, crying, but I didn't look at it. I didn't look at it because I was frozen by another sight. At first, it seemed just another scene from my vivid imagination, only this time I realized I hadn't willed it. I was looking at two creatures curled against a smooth boulder near the sea. They glistened in the sunlight, their lower halves like scales... shiny, reflective. Their upper torsos were soft, pink and smooth like the morning's sunrise, or like the skin on my friend Johnny Wyman's baby sister. Motionless, mesmerized, my eyes wide with wonder, I simply and silently mouthed one word: 'mermaids'. One of the creatures was running her hands through her long black hair. Her back was arched, her head tipped back. Then she shook her head, and ran her hands through her hair again. I looked at her whole body, up and down, over and over, my eyes each time skidding to a stop at her breasts. I looked at her face, and thought of the paintings of angels I'd seen at the museum, faces smooth and rosy with the kind of pink that comes from being a bit embarrassed.

But the tail. It *was* a tail, and it was bent around, partly under a rock, where the other creature, who looked about the same, lay curled up, perhaps sleeping. It was all too much for a little boy, and I backed away slowly. They were probably 150 feet off, and hadn't heard or seen me. Never taking my eyes off of them, I backed around the corner of protruding rock and jutting shore that protected the cove until the mermaids were out of sight. Then I leaned against the ledge, took a deep breath, closed my eyes, counted to ten, and looked around the corner again. They were still there.

And then, as I always did, I ran.

Actually seeing two mermaids was all too much for me to understand. Who in the world would ever believe me? Talking about it with humans was going to get me nowhere; even as a nine year old I knew that. No, I knew where I had to go, and I hurried along back to the beach and the dinghy, and rowed back to Dad's cruising cutter.

Dad was busy up on the bow, cleaning up after putting a coat of varnish on the forward hatch. He looked over his shoulder. "Beachcombing good Pal?" he asked as I climbed aboard the old cutter, and hurried below, uttering a quick 'Oh, fine, Dad." I worked my way forward past the galley, with its black iron Shipmate stove, through the main salon and then the forward cabin until I reached the door of the anchor locker. The small door had an old rusty horseshoe on its face, which Dad had put there way back in 1949 when the boat was launched. The door gave access to an opening through which only a small boy could crawl. But it led to a world of isolation and insulation from the outside world, a world which was away from the cruelty of sixth grade bullies and disbelieving adults. It led to a world usually filled with soothing gurgling sounds, the cool dampness of aged wood, the smell of manila anchor rode, an undulating motion, and a half light that, to this nine year old, somehow felt like a protective cloak. But what was much more important was who lived there. It was the home of an ancient oak wizard: the Stem. I crawled in, and sat there and waited, peering forward into the true darkness of the bow, where the mahogany planks met the great wooden, sea-parting, guiding timber that held much of the boat together, while leading the way through the seas. I heard Dad's scuffing on the deck above while he worked with the anchor line. Still, I waited; perhaps ten minutes. And then, when a slight tidal surge began to lift the old cutter slightly, I heard that noise I wanted to hear; it came from the very farthest point forward. Stem was awake. I leaned forward into the darkness, I could just make out the cracked face of the aged oak, the wise curve of the stem as it turned up to tie in the planks of the bow.

"I saw mermaids, Stem. Two of them. They were girls on top, and fishes on the bottom." Then I heard Dad coming down the forward hatch.

"This will be our secret, Stem" I whispered. I turned and crawled out, through the narrow space, and into the light of another world, a world where there are no such things a mermaids.

The next morning the new east wind brought cold. Wearing heavy sweaters, Dad and I sat in the cockpit drinking our orange juice, and watched as a breeze began to develop from the northeast. "That's not a good sign, Pal, a northeast breeze building this early in the morning in Maine in the summer. Wind could pick up pretty good." He poured some milk on my Rice Crispies. "We should get an early start today." I looked up at the canvas sun awning as it began to come alive for the first time since we'd been in this harbor. But mermaids, not wind, were on my mind.

"Would there be time for me to row ashore? Just one more time for beachcombing?"

"Well, I think it best if I row you in, with this building wind and all. Finish up your cereal, grab you life jacket and we'll go right away. Then we should head back toward Camden."

Then I remembered. My heart sank. "Dad, I'm sorry, I must have left my lifejacket ashore, near the spot where I'd beached the dinghy yesterday. Pleeeeese, just one more time ashore. You like the beach too."

"Well, go get one of the adult lifejackets from under the port bunk. It's too big for you, so just hang on tight to it, OK? I'll row."

When we were about halfway to shore, the breeze began to pick up again, and the newly formed following seas started to smack the dinghy's transom. I felt the cold fingers of spray on my back as I sat in the stern looking forward to the beach.

"Don't move too far to one side; stay in the middle of the seat," Dad said. Even to this day, I remember that rare edge to his voice, that tone of emerging anxiety. I looked down at the accumulated bilge water around my feet, and watched it search for the slightest downward slope, which was toward the very stern corners of the dinghy. The chop was now building such that waves were threatening to overwhelm the corners of the stern. We were midpoint in our journey; the shore and *Phyllis* were now each about one hundred yards away from us.

"I'm going to turn back," Dad said. "STAY STILL AND IN THE MIDDLE OF THE SEAT."

And then he tried to spin the dinghy quickly, pulling on one oar and pushing on the other. And it might have worked if there hadn't been so much water in the dinghy, but the spinning motion sent the bilge water careening to the starboard side, knocking the little boat off balance, and driving one stern corner under, this time to stay. The swamped dinghy settled slowly into the surface of the cove.

My head went under. I popped up. The saltwater, stinging like tears, invaded my nose, my eyes, my senses. I remember blinking, wide-eyed while under water, seeing blurred blue everywhere. I came up again. I flailed, and in doing so I let go of the big adult lifejacket. But my eyes caught sight of Dad, still many yards away but swimming toward me. I went under again. I choked spasmodically, my small body a void the sea was invading. Then I gave in and just stopped fighting. Again, my world turned blurred blue again, confused.

What happened next came from down under, rather than from the surface. Suddenly, I stopped going down and started going up, propelled by a soft, lifting touch on my rear end. I surfaced, choked up seawater, and gasped at the precious air. A short time later an arm came around my neck; it was the big, hairy familiar arm of Dad. "I've got you Pal. I've got you," he said, and he pulled me toward the shore, the waves helping us along. We both crawled up on all fours. I remember Dad lying on his back next to me, his chest heaving. "Are you alright?" he asked.

"Dad, I was going to the bottom! I was going to the bottom! I wasn't going to come up that last time until you pushed me up."

I'll never forget that look on Dad's soaked and shivering face, that questioning look of disbelief at what I'd just said about him pushing me up. He had said nothing, but because of what's happened since in my life, I now know what he must have been thinking. He was thinking he was still ten yards away from me when my head popped to the surface of that cove.

We moved farther up the steep incline of the rocky beach, but as we did so I couldn't help looking back out into the cove. I wasn't sure what I was looking for and not sure what I wanted to see. I did see *Phyllis*; she was beginning to pitch in the still building waves. "We've got to get out of this wind," Dad said. "Otherwise, in this stiff easterly and with us being wet, we'll get hypothermic."

I didn't know what that word meant but it sounded awful, like the needle they put in my mother when she was so sick. I knew then that it was to make her better, but it hadn't, and I hadn't trusted needles ever since. I began to shiver and glanced over at Dad. He was looking toward some big boulders and large fallen pine trees.

"Come on, Davey," he said, "we'll get out of the wind over there, then figure out what to do." We started to climb the rocky beach toward our shelter, when he too turned to look back at Phyllis. Then he stopped and just stared. "She's dragging, Pal," he said.

"How do you know?"

"She's not headed into the seas. It means her anchor is dragging."

I looked as Phyllis's six tons of wood and lead turned slowly broadside to the wind. I could hear the mainsail and jib halyards frantically slapping her fifty foot mast in protest, and I knew the anchor line must be stretching tighter and tighter around the big cleat on deck, as old Phyllis yanked on it, like a relentless dog at a pant leg. The wind began to swing farther to the Northeast, turning the cove from a sheltered anchorage to a vulnerable, unprotected opening facing the fury of the North Atlantic.

Dad spread a wrinkled white hand across his face and squeezed the sides of his head between his thumb and little finger, as if he was either thinking hard for a solution or just hiding his eyes from the sight of *Phyllis* dragging. The wind blew angrily into our faces, watering our eyes. The great pines behind us began to groan and swish their long, needle-filled arms. I imagined *Phyllis's* weight pulling on the big Herreshoff anchor as it slid along the bottom of the cove. I knew there would be no wind down there and it would be oddly quiet. Down there on the bottom, I thought, it wouldn't look like a struggle at all, but more of a private, subtle, slow motion battle. Like a climber slipping off a mountain side, the anchor would try in vain to hook one of its arm-like flukes on a firmly embedded rock. I had always thought of that anchor as another protector, like the stem. Its long iron shank and silver painted flukes had worked as one to keep us from drifting into dangers at night, while we lay in our cozy bunks off of small islands and rocky shores on the coast of Maine. The anchor had never dragged. Now it was dragging, and it seemed the worst time ever. I looked back at Dad; he had removed his hand from his face. He looked up and down the beach and at the water by the shore. "I can't see the swamped dinghy anywhere Pal. It's probably just under the surface somewhere out there. And the oars...the oars aren't in sight either."

"Then what can we do Dad?" I asked. "You have a plan. I know you do. You always have a plan."

"If I can get to *Phyllis*, and then climb aboard, I can start the engine, take the strain off the anchor, motor upwind, and then try to re-set it." He looked out at *Phyllis*. "She's getting closer now; close enough to swim to, I think." His voice was uncertain. "I don't know, I just don't know. But we need shelter, we need dry clothes, we need warmth before nightfall. We need *Phyllis* for that. If I can't save her, then I'll ride ashore with her, but I'll have put together dry clothes, blankets, flares and some food and water in that water-proof canvas abandon ship bag. I'll get off and wade ashore before she breaks up." He looked over at me, his eyes steady. "I can lose *Phyllis*, but I can't lose you."

"But we can't lose me *or* you, Dad," I said, getting frantic now and speaking through chattering teeth. I began to whimper at the thought of losing him, the thought of another void in my life, something again gone that shouldn't be. "It's too rough and too cold. You stay here. Ashore. We can run around and around and get warm. That always works. Don't go."

Dad smiled at me and put a hand on my wet hair. "Works for awhile Pal, but I, and even you, can't run all night." He looked back at *Phyllis*. "Keep an eye on me, but do not go in the water. Ok?" He paused and took a deep breath and stuck out his hand to me. "Ok Pal? Shake on it. I need a solemn pledge: even if you lose sight of me, you will not go in the water."

Dad looked again at *Phyllis*; then he began to remove his khaki pants, shoes and heavy sweater. When he'd done that he said, "I'm keeping my shirt on; it's a trade off; it will slow down my swimming and make it harder to pull myself on board, but it's wool and wool helps retain body warmth when wet."

"But Dad what will I do? If something bad happens? You have to tell me what would I do."

"You survive; that's what you do. Understand? You go up by those pine trees and boulders and pull off as many branches as you can, then you yank as much as you can of that shore grass and hay that's growing behind those trees, then you find a place between the boulders that's out of the wind, then you put down all that hay for a bed, and then you pull as many pine branches over you as you can."

"Dad, please, just don't go. Ok? We can both make a bed up there and keep together for warmth."

He put his hands on my shoulder and looked into my eyes. "Look, if I can't make it to *Phyllis*, I'll swim back and that's what we'll do."

And with that he turned and walked toward the surf. I watched as he waded into the breaking chop at the beach's edge, pushed off, and began stroking his way toward *Phyllis*. The skin of his balding head began to blend with the white foam of the waves, but I could still see the red of his wool shirt with each stroke of his arms. I started running back and forth along the beach to keep warm, my head turned sideways to the sea and my eyes fixed on the flashes of red. At first he made good progress; then he seemed to slow. I began to run faster, back and forth down a short stretch of the beach, as if that would help him pick up his pace. But he slowed more. Then he stopped and tried to float on his back to rest. It was something he'd taught me to do. But it was too rough and he weighed too much in the shirt and the waves crashed over him. I started to yell: "Dad, come back. Come back in to shore. It's too far."

But he turned over and began to swim again toward *Phyllis*. He made slow progress, but as he got closer it got easier in the lee of the boat, which moved slowly sideways while it dragged its anchor. Finally he reached *Phyllis* and hung on to the rudder. As she bounced in the seas so did Dad, his head sometimes going under. "Pull yourself up. Pull yourself up Dad," I yelled against the wind. But he just hung there, exhausted. Then he tried to reach up to the rail of the old cutter, but it was too high and he sank back into the sea.

I started to run again, frantic. "Dad, Dad, Dad" was all I could say, as if, by not letting go of his name, I wouldn't be letting go of him. He popped up again and began to swim along the lee side of *Phyllis* toward the bow. When he got to the anchor line I saw the red sleeve of his wool shirt connect to it, and Dad hung there, being pulled up and down by the changing tension of the line as *Phyllis's* bow rose and fell to the seas. *Phyllis* had a bowsprit, which stuck out ahead of the bow and was connected by a wire, which Dad called a 'bob stay', running from its tip down to a bolt on the waterline part of the Stem. It was another of the Stem's jobs, to hold tight to this wire which kept the bowsprit from being pulled up and broken from the pressure on the head stay when the forward sail was up. Dad had explained the simple physics of this to me one summer, and on one calm and hot day when we were sailing lightly but in a big ocean swell, he'd let me 'ride the bobstay'. Wearing my life jacket and with a line tied to my waist, he'd let me climb out to the tip of the bowsprit and then slide down the bobstay until I was sitting in the nook of where the stay connected to Stem at the waterline. As *Phyllis* rose and fell in the huge swell, I would dip with her, sometimes submerging but always riding back up with the bow as *Phyllis* lifted. It was, to me, the ultimate carnival ride. Now I realized it was having another use. Dad was going to use the wire as a way to get himself aboard. He hooked one leg over the bobstay and rested there, his hands hanging farther up the wire toward the tip of the bowsprit. I watched, frozen now by the beach's edge, as he clung suspended like one of those zoo animals that hang upside down from a branch. He just hung there until it seemed certain he would have to let go. Then, when a larger rolling sea came and lifted *Phyllis's* bow, he put one foot in the crook where the bobstay was bolted to the Stem and hung on while lifted out of the water as she rose up with the sea. As the roller passed and *Phyllis* descended, burying her bow, he let the sea lift him up, giving him enough buoyancy to roll and hook himself over the top of the bowsprit. Then he crawled aft and disappeared into the cabin. Soon I saw a puff of exhaust and I knew he had her engine running. Dad came right back on deck, this time wearing a heavy white sweater. *Phyllis* began to turn toward the seas as he put the engine in forward and took the strain of the dragging anchor. "All right Dad!" I cheered, now hopping up and down rather than running back and forth on the beach. Over the next ten minutes I watched him move *Phyllis* ahead for short stretches, then run forward and take in the excess anchor line, then repeat the process until he was able to get the old Herreshoff anchor free of the sea and hanging over the tip of the bowsprit. Next he motored *Phyllis* farther out in the cove and reset the anchor. He waited in the cockpit to see if she dragged. Then he went into the cabin. I waited. I began to shiver uncontrollably and started to yell for him. The wind was still strong and I realized I didn't know the next part of the plan. Dad hadn't told me. He must have one, I thought. Dad always had a plan for everything. Then I saw him emerge with something big and yellow. I realized it was the dry bag he'd shown me several times. It was one of the first ones made, and Dad had bought it from an outfitter who led rafting expeditions. It became our abandon ship waterproof bag, stuffed with a whistle, a signaling mirror, flares, a water jug, waterproof matches, dry clothes, and a blanket. Dad reached into the bag, pulled out the whistle and blew it and waved. He had my attention. He stood on the stern and blew the whistle, waved his arms and pointed to the bag. I waved back. He blew the whistle again and made a gesture like he was throwing the bag into the water. He waved his arms a second time. I waved back. Then he blew the whistle a third time, loud and long, and heaved the bag toward shore. I waved back. I waited anxiously while the waves in the cove slowly carried the rescue bag ashore. I ran to it as it grounded out, as if it were my 'big present' from Christmas, and pulled it up the beach and into the high grass between the boulders. It yielded a pair of corduroy pants, my thick red wool sweater and a blue wool watch cap. I put on the cap, laid out the sweater and pants on the grass, quickly stripped down and then climbed into the dry clothes. I dug back into the bag, found a wool red and white striped blanket, and wrapped it around me. Then I walked out from between the big boulders and looked for Dad and *Phyllis*. The old cutter wasn't rocking as much and the choppy waves in the cove had begun to flatten. *Phyllis's* anchor appeared to be holding, and I could just make out Dad huddled in the cockpit under another of our red and white striped blankets. It was then that I spied the swamped dinghy; it had washed ashore and was just now visible on the beach to my right, its bow and stern just poking the surface of the calming seas. I jumped up and down, running to the water's edge and yelling to Dad while pointing at it with one hand and holding the blanket around me with the other. The oars couldn't be far away, I thought. But first I waded in a few feet, leaving the blanket dry on the beach, and pulled the bow up as far as I could on shore. It wasn't far, but it would be enough. I could tell by the seaweed and wet rocks on the beach that the tide was going out, and the dinghy would soon be high and dry. I began my search for the oars. It didn't take long; one was washed ashore not far away. I never found the other, but I knew one would be enough. The hardest part of the process was now emptying the dinghy, but by rocking it back and forth, I sloshed enough water out to be able to roll it over and empty it fully. Now the wind was dying quickly, and I was able to paddle out to Dad and *Phyllis*. It was a great reunion. Giving Dad a hug, patting old *Phyllis*, and getting one big cup of hot chocolate — all this brought calm. We sat in silence for awhile, Dad staring blankly at the empty water off *Phyllis*'s bow. Then he looked at me.

"I don't understand. I just don't understand. I had no strength. No strength at all. No adrenaline even." He cocked his head, as if confused by his own statement.

"Then I think you must have had some help, Dad," was all I said. And then, while he rubbed his temples and stirred his cocoa, I headed into the cabin, forward, to talk with Stem about watching for mermaids.

EPILOG — 51 YEARS LATER

It's 2011.
My life is sixty years long now —
fifty-one years since I first saw the mermaids.
I still watch for them.
It doesn't matter that they haven't reappeared.
What really matters, after all, is the watching.
And the wondering.

WHEN NO ONE ELSE
IS WATCHING

As we rounded the point, the fog came right back. Just then I caught the first smell of spruce and felt the warmth of the land. Despite the fog, I looked for the entrance to the cove, eager to end that day's foggy sail into an unrelenting southwest headwind. Soon I could do my favorite things: some rowing in the old skiff and then exploring a calm new place.

"The old cruising guide says the entrance is hard to spot, between the cliffs just beyond this point; it says we should look for a bold, pink granite cliff on the eastern side," my father said. I watched Dad now. I looked at him only for intent. Not with fear or anxiety. My father would not make a mistake.

"Grab that red cardboard megaphone, behind the port bunk, will you pal?" my father asked. "We'll make our own radar."

I dove into the cabin, grabbed the megaphone, and handed it to my father, who put it to his lips. "Boom....boom....boom," he shouted through the megaphone at different intervals and in slightly varied directions. He waited and did it again. Curious, I watched intently. "Seems as if the much longer return echo is right about there," he said, pointing into the fog while looking down at the binnacle. "About 20 degrees." He let go the staysail sheet and the old wooden cutter slowed appreciably. "We'll just ease on closer and listen very carefully for surf," he said. "Why don't you take those sharp eyes and good ears of yours up to the bow and put them to work."

And so we ghosted in toward the entrance. I hung to the fore-stay, my left foot resting on the bowsprit, while I unleashed my full senses of sight and sound. Then I spied it. "There, Dad... there. There's the pink cliff, just like you said. Just like you said Dad."

He was probably immensely relieved, though he didn't show it outwardly. I'm sure he was nowhere near as certain of himself as I was of him. And there were more worries to come. "Come get the lead line for me, will you pal?" he asked, as we slid through the entrance. I came aft, grabbed the lead line from the stern locker, unwound it to three knots, which I knew meant three fathoms, or eighteen feet, and moved forward dutifully to just aft of the starboard running backstay. "Ok, begin your swings," Dad said, and I swung the lead forward into the water and let it drop as the cutter moved ahead. "No bottom," I said. And I swung again. "Still no bottom."

"All good," Dad said, as we eased by the bold shore with the pink granite cliff. "We're almost in. About a hundred yards farther, and we should be inside the cove and you'll pick up the bottom on the lead line. When you do, I'll round up and we'll drop anchor."

Several hours later, when the fog lifted, we were surprised to find that we were not alone. A large cabin cruiser was anchored not far off. Dad seemed surprised; since we'd left Massachusetts, we'd seen very few big power boats at anchor in remote coves. He began reheating a beef stew we'd had the night before. I was happy to climb into the rowing skiff and explore the shoreline. Rowing back from the other side of the cove, my curiosity got the better of me about the man on the cabin cruiser, and I rowed over near the neighboring cruiser. A large man was sitting in the stern, his feet propped up on the transom. He was smoking a cigar and drinking a beer. I thought the better of getting closer, but as I turned, the man stood up and looked in my direction.

"Hey boy...know where we are here, boy?" he asked. "We kind of stumbled in here as the fog started. Been stuck for a couple of days."

"It's called Head Harbor," I said. "It's on the chart. My dad brought us in here right through the fog. Right in. He knows the place."

"Thanks," the man said, and settled back in his chair.

After dinner, I went below decks to read and my father, after cleaning the dishes, sat up on deck with a cup of tea. It was dusk and very quiet. Then came a rustle of small objects and a series of small splashes. The noise came from the direction of the other boat in the cove. Dad turned and watched as the man on the power boat dumped his trash over the stern of his boat into the still waters of the pristine harbor.

"I'm going for a short row, pal," Dad said. He put down his tea by the rail, and slid over the side into the skiff.

Very deliberately, he rowed toward the other boat in the cove. As he got closer, the man in the stern took notice. He sat up straighter, stopped leaning back in his chair, and then took his feet down from the boat's transom. He put down his beer. Then he put down his cigar. But Dad slowed the skiff and turned before reaching the cabin cruiser. He was about sixty feet off, near the slowly spreading pool of garbage. Then he shipped his oars and began to pick the various pieces of the jetsam out of the water. Carefully, slowly, he picked up a soup can with its ragged lid partially attached, a cardboard egg carton, four beer bottles, a coffee can, and numerous candy bar wrappers. He placed each item in a canvas bucket in the stern of our skiff. The man on the cabin cruiser watched, motionless, at full attention. I watched, motionless, at full attention. Dad rowed slowly toward the man. In the stillness of the cove, no one said a word. The only sound came from the skiff's old ash oars as they sliced the water and pulled toward the man's boat. Dad rounded up the skiff nicely alongside the cabin cruiser's stern. Then he stood, bucket in hand, and poured its contents at the man's feet.

"I think you may have dropped this," was all he said. And then he rowed away.

They say that 'character' is what you do when no one else is watching. In this case, a young boy watched. So did an older man. Neither, I venture, has ever been the same.

II

YOUTH

Harnessed to False Security

"Hope for the Best, but Plan for the Worst." A famous round-the-world sailor has this imprinted on his companionway bulkhead. I guess he did it as a constant reminder about using good judgment. Makes sense. Those of us with a few miles under our keels know that things can very quickly go from sublime to terrifying, even <u>with</u> good planning.

With kids there's a bigger problem. The part of the brain that deals with consequences isn't very well developed. Remember responding to that "double dare" as a kid? Remember looking down off that ledge or that railroad bridge on that hot summer's day and feeling pressure from your peers overcoming your basic survival instincts? Many of us jumped. Stupid.

I remember responding to such a double dare from two friends while zooming along in a 13 foot Boston Whaler outboard at the age 13. "Stand up in the bow Roper; see if you can hang on while we spin out at full throttle," came the dare. I took the bait; friend Robbie whipped the wheel hard to starboard, and the boat spun around. In just two or three seconds, three things happened: (1) I flew through the air; (2) for some odd reason I started laughing while in the air and then underwater; and (3) I opened my eyes to see a propeller whip by my face. As I swam toward my friends on the fast-returning boat, I no longer felt immortal.

When I was 17, after being inspired by teenaged solo circum-navigator Robin Lee Graham, I decided I should do something like he did, but on a much smaller scale. So I set sail alone toward Nantucket. I did it in a 23-foot True Rocket centerboard cabin sloop of questionable breed. I'd purchased it for $2,500 with funds earned while working at a shoe factory. I was about to head off at last, on the verge of becoming the next famous teenage sailor. I knew, however, that I must always be prepared for the worst, while still looking cool.

So what I needed was a lifesaving harness. A justifiably concerned friend of my father's gave me his old one. It was more of a fat canvas belt than a harness, like something a jackhammer operator would wear around his stomach. But to me, it was cool. I pictured making each port alone and salt encrusted, tethered to my noble vessel, while teenaged tourist maidens swooned from their shore side perches at every move of the romantic young adventurer.

The second day of my voyage, while drifting along a couple miles off Plymouth on a course toward the Cape Cod Canal, I decided to test out my harness. I was planning for the worst, and I wanted to practice. I snapped the tether's big brass clip to a shroud, leaned out over the windward side, let go both hands, spread my arms, put my full weight on the manila rope tether, and imagined myself fighting for survival in a horrific storm off Cape Horn. Unfortunately, it was a *manila* rope tether (manila rope rots); it wasn't Super Spectra, Torlon, Zargon, carbon-fiber, or any other mega strength synthetic non-rotting rope tether.

What happened next I have never disclosed to anyone; you're the first, gentle or crusty reader, though by now I'm sure you can guess. Yes, the ancient manila rope broke and I back-flopped into the sea. My 23-foot True Rocket (which, thankfully, was never anything close to a rocket) lumbered away from me. When I surfaced, my first thought, oddly, was not one of survival, but of gratitude that no one was watching. I swam easily to my Wal-Mart-quality rubber raft that followed faithfully astern, rolled into it and pulled myself back to the mother ship.

The voyage continued for 36 days that summer. There was one maiden, though her swoon soon faded. I got lost at sea in the fog. I got real scared. I got lonely. I ran out of money. But, like Robin Lee Graham, I continued on alone. And I was cool, because, until now, no one was the wiser.

BEHIND HER MONA LISA SMILE

She sat before me in all her 21 year-old splendor. She looked relaxed, as if she were enjoying the coolness that came with the late summer afternoon. Her hair was cut short. She combed it with her fingers now, tilting her head back while putting every wind-blown strand in place.

And my 17 years sat before her, quiet and motionless except for an occasional wince from the pain of my sunburned forehead. I leaned back, surveying the horizon like an old salt at the end of a dying day. The true intent of the gesture, however, was to peripherally catch a glimpse of her tiny white shorts and the long tan legs that flowed so wondrously out of them. I didn't think of her perspective. I was 17. I didn't realize that it was not too late for the setting sun to show the peach fuzz of a beard on my face. I didn't realize that the tufts of curly red hair that sprouted from under the band of my dirty white tennis hat —which I had put on much too late in the day — made me look like a sun-baked cabbage patch character.

It didn't seem necessary for us to talk now. I figured that now was an accepted period of contemplation over the beauty of the sail we'd just had. And she may have been thinking of that. I definitely was not.

We'd anchored in an isolated little cove, not far from an island with a flat sandy beach that partially rimmed my small cruising sloop. It was a good, safe anchorage and we had things all to ourselves.

"Most everyone will have to be back to the rat race tomorrow morning," I said finally. I wondered if I had broken a silence that I shouldn't have. I couldn't be too careful.

She turned to me and smiled. "But not you, Dave. Not the roving sailor."

"And you," I asked. "When do you have to be back?"

"Not 'til three o'clock."

"Tomorrow?"

"I hope so. It's way after three o'clock today."

My thoughts raced. She spoke: "Dave, where did you get the money to buy this cute little boat?"

I'd never thought of it "cute". "It cost me $2500, and I earned every cent of it myself, pumping gas all last summer in a marina. My dream ever since I can remember has been to buy a boat and sail up and down the Massachusetts coast by myself."

"And you're halfway now," she said.

"Yeah, though sometimes I wonder if I'll ever get out of Hyannis. People have been so nice."

"Were those some of your college friends from Hyannis at the party the other night?"

"Well, mostly, yeah, college friends." I hurried it along. "And you? You're just here for the summer fun?"

"Just here for the summer fun. I've been coming every summer since freshman year. I think I told you at the party, but I go to Ohio State. And you said you went where?"

My mind raced and landed on the only college I could think of. "Union. Union College." (It was my older brother's school).

She looked at me now and cocked her head a little. "Just started? Got a major yet?'

"Me? Just started? No. God no, I'm a junior. Well, junior this coming year."

"Oh, I could have sworn...wow, it was so loud at that party."

"No, I don't think we got that far. I mostly told you about sailing," I said.

"So what is your major?" she asked.

"Psychology."

"Terrific. My major too! We do have a lot to talk about. I'm afraid, however, that I'm an old lady. Be graduating this coming May."

"No problem," I said. "I like older women." And then I winked at her.

She smiled slightly, cocked her head, and leaned toward me, her face near mine. Over her shoulder, I glimpsed a small piece of the day's sun lingering over the beach. My palms started to sweat. "You'd make a cute little brother," she said.

That hurt. It made me angry. *Little brother... I ought to stand up and show her what I got.*

"I didn't mean that in an intimidating way, David," she said, finally. *David*, I thought. *David*. No one ever called me David, except that old fart of a guidance counselor this year at high school. I offered her a beer.

"No, thank you."

"I think I'll have one." I grabbed for the six pack in the cooler under the cockpit seat. It felt like a secret weapon, a teenager's spinach, a last shot to make me brave. My mind scanned the previous few minutes. *Cute little brother...but then again, she'd called me a "roving sailor"...she'd accepted my offer to come on the boat at that party. And now she was five miles from civilization, with the sun going down. And three o'clock tomorrow, she'd said. Tomorrow. One hell of a long date.* I was smug again.

I downed the first beer and popped the top of another. She didn't seem to notice; she was looking at the water. It was getting dark now, and quiet. The wind was gone and the water had ceased patting and was now rubbing the white sides of the boat. I wondered what she was thinking. I gulped from my beer, feeling the biting bubbles on my throat. The words of a seemingly profound sentence about the night's serenity came to my lips, but then I thought the words would seem phony. "Nice night," came out instead.

"Oh, yes, things are so... so passive and serene," she said.

Again I drank deeply from my beer, as if courage lay at the bottom of the can. I thought about constructing another sentence, something about the gloriousness of sail, something about nature's breath being idyllic propulsion. *There's some syllables*, I thought.

"I think I will have a beer now," she said softly. But I was preoccupied with 'idyllic propulsion'. For a moment I didn't answer. "Never mind, I'll get it," she said. She leaned over my lap to reach for a beer. Suddenly she was all face, up close. "Let's swim ashore and go for a walk after I finish the beer," she said. My hand clutched tight to the cockpit seat. "Great," I chirped. She pulled on the tab of the can, and then moved to a prone position on the cockpit floor. I watched her there, her eyes closed and a slight smile on her lips. I looked at her tight white shorts and my mind had us swimming, naked, ashore. Then a huddle for warmth. Warming her. Shoulders stretched big to protect. Bodies close. Touching. And then a long kiss. Mouths then cheeks then hugs. And beautiful unhurried love made on the sand. And afterwards her head on my shoulder. In my lightheadedness I spoke, "We'll take the rest of the *sex*-pack with us."

"What?"

"Six-pack. Beer. We'll bring it with us."

"Oh," she said. She had that half smile again.

My palms were still sweating and I wiped them on my cut off jeans. There was a long pause and I didn't know what to do next. I knew I needed more beer, more time.

"Tell me of some of the places you've been since you left home?" she asked.

"Oh. Lots of stops. The usual places."

"Like where?"

"Just places down the coast. You know."

"I don't. I really don't. That's precisely the point. I don't live around here, remember?"

"That's right. I keep forgetting. Well, I've been to Nantucket, Martha's Vineyard, Plymouth, and a whole mess of little harbors."

"Do you know people along the way?"

"Some places." There was another long pause. She looked into me carefully.

"Wanna go to the beach now?" I asked.

"How come you don't want to just sit and talk?"

"I do. Really. I just thought you wanted to go on the beach, that's all. You do, don't you?"

"Yes, but not this minute."

"Okay. I just wanted to know."

"Now you know."

"Yup."

We sat for what seemed like a long time, just looking at the sky. Soon the stars began to pop into view. I became worried. I was worried that it would get too cold for swimming soon. I was worried about how I was handling things. I was worried about this 'little brother' business. I looked over at her in the dwindling light. She was running her forefinger around the top of her can of beer while staring at the stars. I looked where she was staring. "That's Venus, the evening star," I said.

"I don't know the stars. You've given me a real treat by sharing all this with me today David."

"This is my world," I said easily. "I suppose it's different back in Ohio. I mean, same stars and all, just different."

"That's why I come here for the summers. I guess the sun and the sand and the sea help fortify me for the coming year at school. It's nice."

"Then why keep going back to Ohio?"

She put the beer down and turned on her side, leaned on one elbow, and looked at me. "It's my home. It's where I was raised. Just like this is where you were raised."

I smiled, and tilted my head at her. "Yeah, but isn't Ohio kind of, you know, well ... ugly?"

She sat up. She was upset. "Now look David ..."

My face prickled and I realized I'd made a mistake, my second. "I just asked. That's all. Look, I don't know. I don't know. I just heard. That's all."

"Well, don't believe all you hear."

"I don't."

"Well, okay. I think a person should always go out and see places, and things, before going around and commenting about them."

I leaned forward, trying to be compassionate. "Look, I was only trying to kid you a little. Of course I don't know anything about Ohio."

She smiled. "I guess I'm just a little touchy about my home state."

"Yeah, sorry."

Our part of the earth was rapidly losing its heat from the day. Now, if it happened at all, it would be a cold swim. Already she had put her shoulders closer together and leaned forward in an attempt to keep warm before going to her sweater. If I were in Tahiti, like my world-roaming sailing hero Peter Tangvald, I thought, there wouldn't be this problem. Tangvald probably had some girl on the beach with him right now. He would have moved faster, saying just the right lines, and would have had her over the side, swimming naked ashore. He wouldn't have to deal with New England weather. Hell, I thought, the only thing you have to deal with in Paradise is eating too much breadfruit.

She was staring at the stars again. I thought some more about Tangvald, how he'd given up his steady job ashore and kissed it all off and headed where the wind would take him. I thought of his courage, his confidence with women, and of all the places he had been.

"Look, I'm sorry too," she said suddenly. "Tell me more about your world and your dreams."

"My dream is to follow in the footsteps, or I should say 'wakes' of some of my heroes."

"What heroes?"

Guys like Tangvald, Slocum, Moitessier."

"Who are these people?"

I told her about Joshua Slocum being the first person to sail alone around the world. I told her how independent and resourceful he was, having rebuilt an abandoned oyster sloop by himself in his later years, sailing it through the oceans alone, and even escaping cannibals in the Pacific.

"How did he do that?"

"He sprinkled tacks on his decks at night; when the cannibals slipped aboard and climbed over the rail, they were sent screaming over the side into the water, their bare feet filled with the sharp tacks."

She seemed really interested now. "And Moitessier?"

"He just couldn't get enough of the sea. He signed up for a solo around-the-world sailboat race with a big cash prize. For seven months, he battled storms, doldrums, gear failures, and knockdowns, as well as fatigue and loneliness. Then, nearing the finish with victory at hand, he suddenly pulled out of the race and sailed on, relaying word that the prize money meant nothing to him anymore. He'd found something more important at sea."

"So he stayed at sea?

"For another three months. Ended up in Tahiti."

"So that's what you want to do? That's your dream. To sail around and around at sea?"

"I'd be free as a bird, able to make choices in my own world."

She thought for a minute, and I watched her. I felt the wind shifting; a light breeze began to drift onto us from the mainland. "Yes, I agree, but you don't have to be out there, on a sailboat, to make choices. I mean, there can't <u>be</u> many choices out there, right?"

"I don't see what you mean."

"Well, it seems almost like it would be all instinctual out there... survival, day by day. Seems like we've evolved past that in our society. Seems like we all know we'll survive, from one day to the next anyway, and because of this our existence has taken on another meaning, another raison d'etre, so to speak. And going back out there, around and around, would be like reverting to that primitive level, don't you think?"

I didn't have the faintest idea what she was talking about, though I rose immediately to my heroes' defense. "These guys are out there living their dream, doing what millions of people dream about: quitting the rat race, breathing the clean air, creating their own world." I smiled at her, and looked at my beer. "Grabbing for gusto, as the beer people say."

She was quiet. I thought maybe she was put off again.

"It seems you have to define 'gusto'," she said, finally. "And I think that is kind of like defining art. Very hard to do. There are so few of these people, these heroes of yours David that...".

"There are always too few heroes," I interjected. "Look at all the dreamers behind them, the people who wish they could go."

"Then why don't they?"

"Lots of reasons: family, job security, debts."

She was thinking again, and I became more and more uneasy. I didn't want to get into an argument. I didn't want to discuss this. I wanted that swim, or at least what came after that swim.

She continued. "I guess it seems you've got to do a lot of defining, so as to at least understand the basics, the basic drive. We should define words like 'gusto' and 'hero' and 'dream'. What are they in today's world?"

I reached into the cooler and opened a beer. *Basic drive*, I thought. *I'll define basic drive for you.*

"Don't you think so?" she asked again.

"Yeah, I guess you're right," I said, rubbing the peach fuzz on my chin, trying to look thoughtful. I had no idea where she was going with this.

"Let's define 'dream'," she said.

I took a pull on my beer. *Let's go swimming. Naked.* I thought.

She scratched her forehead. "Are you saying your heroes' dreams are manifest in all of us?"

I looked her in the eyes. "I wonder," I said, not quite sure what 'manifest' meant.

"So do I, David. Which leads me on. Can a dream ever be a reality? Can a dream ever be achieved? Doesn't it lose everything it is, in essence, when it is realized? Again, I wonder."

"Hmmmmm."

"Really, it follows logically that a dream can't be achieved." She sighed. I understood this much: she had just called my life a fantasy.

She continued. "Ever study Freud? His theories state that dreams have a manifest content — the conscious experience during sleep, the dream that we remember — and a latent content. He proposed that the latent dream content is composed of three elements: the sensory impressions during the night; the residues of the previous day; and the id's instinctive drives. During sleep, the repression by the super-ego is weakened due to the absence of voluntary motor activity; this increases the possibility of instinctive impulses reaching consciousness."

"I see," I said. (I didn't). Jesus, I thought, she really *studied* psychology.

"Well, anyway," she continued. "we agree on a premise — that a dream is something not yet achieved. It is something that has its greatest power, its greatest drive, in its latent state. It is something that is not tarnished by any of the pitfalls of reality. It is not happening. It is imagined. Therefore, it is not a reality. For a dream to be achieved, it has to become a reality. Right? And since something that is not real isn't, then a dream cannot be. See?"

Between the beer and my limited high school education, I knew I was in heavy cross seas. But I felt attacked. I wanted to defend my romance, my dream. "I think that if you stop and define things all the time, you get caught up in words and get nowhere. At least I'm headed somewhere. At least I have a goal. You're saying my life is nothing." I was poised, ready to give up the naked swimming. I was ready to fight.

She sensed it. "I'm sorry," she said, and she turned slightly from her position on the cockpit floor and leaned her head on my knee. I melted. My arm came down and I began to smooth her hair with my hand, and then I combed it a little with my fingers.

"Look, this is no fun," I said. We'll just talk in circles and that never gets anywhere. You know, good old Cape Cod's Gulf Stream water is probably warmer than its air right now. How about that swim?" She said nothing, but seemed relaxed. I continued. "Just a thought. I've got a waterproof tube of matches. I could bring them ashore and we'll burn some driftwood. Start a fire. It would be nice and we'd be warm in no time."

She stood up quickly and smiled at me. She put her palm on my cheek. "It better start right up, or we'll freeze to death."

And by God if she didn't remove those tight little shorts. I saw flashes of whiter skin in the dark, and dove into the cabin to find the matches. There was a splash, and when I came on deck she was thirty feet from the boat and swimming toward shore. I flew out of my cutoffs and polo shirt and dove in. The water temperature was nothing to write home about. I swam after her with everything I had. The water felt numbing on my body, especially on my sunburned forehead. I was catching her. I'd dive under and grab her legs and pull her under and we'd laugh and hug and kind of kick our way to the beach in each other's arms. That's what we'd do, I thought. Then the cramp hit me. First it came as a nagging pain, deep from within. I slowed down a bit. She was still 30 yards from shore. I had time to slow down. But soon the nagging became stabbing, so that each stroke made me wince. Finally, I had to stop. I tried treading water, with a slight kick to head me to shore, but the cramp immobilized me. I was a good swimmer and knew what to do: I rolled over and floated on my back. The swell rolled me toward the beach, like a dead fish coming in with the tide. She was on shore now, shivering, dancing on her toes, her arms clutched around herself. She stared into the darkness, then shouted. "David? David, come on. Bring the matches. I'm freezing." The cramp eased a bit, and I rolled over and did a very slow breast stroke in to shore, still clutching the tube of matches in my right hand.

"There you are. What took you so long? I was worried. And freezing."

The cramp was still with me, but I tried not to show it, pretending to be doubled up from the shivering, and not the pain. "Kind of cold," I said "Couldn't find the matches at first on the boat. Finally did, though." I held them up in my hand. I wanted to breathe long deep breaths to relieve the cramp, but was afraid it would appear that I was exhausted from the short swim, and out of shape.

"Well, let's get to that fire," she said. "I'll look for wood." And then she disappeared into the night. Our huddle for warmth would be delayed. I walked up the beach a few steps, breathing deeply now, nursing the cramp. Then I stood still, deciding it best not to move for awhile. The pain was back to a nag, but I didn't want it to flare up again. I waited. Then her voice came from the night. "Dave, there's plenty. I found plenty." She appeared, like a ghost emerging from the sand dunes behind her. Her arms were piled with driftwood up to her chin, leaving only her head and torso visible. The sight of her made me think for the first time of our nakedness. I glanced down. I was shriveled up beyond belief. I turned, embarrassed. "I think I saw a good place for the fire down the way a bit. I'll check." I moved off quickly, leaving her carrying the wood. Her voice followed, slightly irritated, asking me to slow down and help carry some of the wood. I came back and took some of the wood from her arms. We moved briskly together toward a spot between two sand dunes. We were both shivering, but the wood was old and dry, and there was hope for the coming warmth. We knelt down in the sand. She stacked the wood in a pyramid; inside it she placed small twigs and a clump of cardboard she'd found. I fumbled with the lid to the matches, finally got it off, and scratched the bottom of the tube with one of the water-proof match sticks. It lit, and then the cardboard lit, and then the twigs and finally the whole pyramid. It all burned beautifully, lighting up our faces while we watched, relieved, while rubbing our hands together. I viewed her through the flames now; she seemed a somehow distant and untouchable apparition amidst the pops and hisses of the burning wood. I didn't know what to do next; I realized I had no more pages in my script. It ended here. What would Tangvald do right now, I wondered. What would he say to her to make it all happen. It was just then that an ember shot from the fire, and landed on her leg. She jumped up and swore a nasty swear. A sailor's swear. I stood. "Are you okay? Are you okay?" She swore again and looked back toward the boat. "This just isn't working, David. I need to go back to the boat *right* away." And with that, she headed down the beach.

With head drooped like an admonished puppy, I followed along through the sand. Maybe, I thought, you just can't plan romance.

SEADUCTION

My age of innocence ended around midnight on a July Saturday in 1969. It happened alongside a cruising yawl named *Seaduction*. What I inadvertently caused to happen, and what I experienced in a few short minutes gave me my first real look at the other side of the adult world.

As a teenager I knew kids could be rascals, but I had never experienced any real impurities or waywardness in grownups, except, perhaps, when I was five and my Dad and I discovered that Mr. Macy had, without asking, taken the oars to our skiff. I still remember the shock I felt when I learned that adults could be sneaky. But that was minor compared to what happened the summer of my 18th year.

Early in that summer of 1969 I had been awarded my first command: operating a 23-foot yacht club harbor launch, shuttling members and visiting guests to and from their yachts. Being a launch driver was a coveted position, especially in the major yachting center of Marblehead, Massachusetts, a small 17th century town harboring some 1,500 yachts, five yacht clubs, and a harbor so big and crowded one could almost be anonymous – almost.

By early July, I was assigned my first 3 p.m. to midnight shift. The afternoon and early evening part went well. During the afternoon, I worked in tandem with a veteran launch driver, and the two of us brought most everyone ashore by sunset. After sunset, however, the other launch boy's shift ended; I would be on my own until midnight. Right around dusk, I was returning from a drop-off of a visiting yachtsman's family at the head of the harbor when a man from a slowly motoring yawl waved me over. "Do you have a guest mooring for the night?" he asked.

The veteran launch boy had primed me for what he called "the classic tip-generating response." I had plenty of moorings available for visitors, as the yacht club's cruise was ongoing and many boats were away. But regardless, I slowly shook my head, clenched my lips, and gave him the most pessimistic and concerned look I could. "Boy, that's tough, sir; pretty tight. Well, let me think." That man looked across at me intently, pleadingly. "Well, there may be a mooring way up at the head of the harbor," I ventured.

"I'll certainly make it worth your while," then man said.

Bingo! "Follow me, I replied, and put my launch in gear. Even though I knew where the mooring was, for a little effect I motored around "searching" for one. Finally, I pointed. "There you go sir; you'll be fine on this one." He waved me over, and I pulled up along his starboard side. Few things are certain in life, but one of them was that there was a big tip coming.

"Here you go," he said, handing me a twenty (a lot of money in 1969!) I was at his service!

"We close at midnight, by the way, in case you want to come ashore I'm glad to take you."

"No, we're fine for the night," he said. Then the man leaned toward me, and gestured toward his money now in my hand. "You never saw this boat tonight, OK?" It was then I noticed an attractive woman standing in the yawl's companionway.

"No problem," I said, and headed back to the yacht club. As I did, I looked back over my shoulder and, in the last moment of dwindling light I could just make out the boat's name: *Seaduction.*

From 9 p.m. until about 11:45, all was quiet in the harbor. I sat in the launch shack at the yacht club, monitoring the radio and waiting for any late-night stragglers. Just before midnight I heard clomping feet, slurred words, and laughter from the gangway behind the shack. It was a group of about eight or nine adults.

They walked past the shack and piled into my launch, which was idling with its running lights on. As I climbed aboard, someone from the group said they were from the *Blue Jacket,* a big powerboat moored at the head of the harbor.

Off we went. A three-quarter moon lit the way pretty well. Still, I had to concentrate to avoid empty mooring buoys and pennants, and not be distracted by the drunken adults standing behind me in the launch. Snagging a mooring at night with a launch half full of people would not go down well with my boss. We made it OK, and I pulled up carefully to the starboard side of *Blue Jacket.* The group climbed out of the launch amid more laughter, a few thanks, but no tip. Oh, well, I'd done alright that night anyway with the *Seaduction* guy. It got me to wondering: What *was* happening right now aboard *Seaduction?*

She was just a few boats over; in fact, without thinking, I must have passed right by her on the way to *Blue Jacket.* Now that I'm alone, I thought, why not cruise by and do a bit of snooping on my way in for the night? I altered course a bit and her stern came into view, as well as the shape of two people, clearly locked in a passionate embrace in the cockpit. That's close enough, I thought, and began to turn. At that moment I felt a tap on my shoulder; my 18-year old heart entered the lower part of my throat.

"Geeze," I yelped. And there, standing in the glow of the launch's stern light, was a woman in a black sweater. She was pointing to the *Seaduction.*

'Right there," she said. Let me out on that boat." She must have been sitting in the stern behind the other group, waiting to tell me her destination until the others were dropped off. Then she must have seen the *Seaduction* as I passed and stood up and pointed.

So now the same launch boy who had received a $20 payoff from the man to stay away, was, like a golden retriever bringing back a rabid squirrel to the feet of its master, depositing this woman — the last person on earth the man wanted to see — at his feet. To put it mildly, it was all quite awkward.

The man looked at me, then at the woman in the launch. I saw the whites of his eyes despite the darkness. Then, in a stark absolute tone, he said: "Gloria." It wasn't "Gloria?" It wasn't "*Gloria!*" It was, like the finality of death, just "Gloria."

"Go below George," Gloria said, as she climbed aboard *Seaduction*. The other woman seemed to melt into the corner of the cockpit. And I? Well, I left the scene. Yes, I left them — all *three* of them — out there together for the night.

So we're all left to wonder: Just what *did* happen on *Seaduction* after midnight. I'll never know. Though George does, and so does Gloria. And so does the other woman. As for me, well, it was then past midnight and I was off the clock. The launch was closed for the night.

And the person who was once a launch "boy" came of age, and headed home, wondering.

Someone's Been Sleeping in My Bed

As a 20-something, I was the captain of a 58-foot wooden schooner in Marblehead. The boat was a classic, but the true character was my boss. He was probably the most unflappable man I ever met. I remember him vividly, sitting casually at the helm of his great schooner, engaged intently in conversation with several guests, a gin and tonic in one hand, a couple of fingers of the other resting on a spoke of the big teak wheel, while taking this huge vessel with her long bowsprit all the way to the head of crowded, tiny Manchester Harbor. I was his "captain" but he was the owner, so I simply crouched quietly by the bits at the bow, bit my tongue and held my breath, as the ten-foot bowsprit whisked past the sterns and bows of several moored boats, missing each and every one by only inches. No one was ever sure if my boss just had an uncanny sense of the control of his big yacht, or if he was just plum lucky every time. But he *always* missed.

He seemed such a care-free man, living for the moment, and never the moment after. One day, back on the mooring, as he looked down into the engine room, he said: "Say, Chief, why don't you give that big old engine a coat of paint tomorrow. It's all gray and black and greasy. And paint it white this time so it's really shiny." When I replied that that was fine, but it would take two days to do it, and he'd miss an extra sailing day, he asked me why the two days. I replied that it would take me one day of prep to degrease and scrape it, and one day to paint. "I don't want to miss *two* days of sailing," he said. "What will happen if you just paint it...just spray the thing white, nice and thick and pretty?" Well, I told him, the paint will fall off. "How soon?" he asked. I told him I didn't know how soon, but eventually it would. "Eventually? What's 'eventually'? Everything that happens, happens eventually. No, just paint it," he said emphatically. "I'll probably be dead before the paint comes off anyway, and this way I won't miss an extra day of sailing."

Anyway, you get the idea about this unflappable man and his living for the moment. Which brings me to his crowning moment of unflappability. I'll set the scene: My boss lived in a huge house right next door to one of the big yacht clubs in Marblehead. It had a long front porch, great foyer with ship models, and a big, winding staircase leading up to the second floor, where the hallway led to several bedrooms, including the guest room. In fact, it was very similar to the front entrance area of the yacht club next door.

One summer an out of town couple came to visit friends who were members of this club. The hosts had arranged for the couple to stay in one of the hotel rooms at the yacht club. That evening, they all had dinner and drinks at the hosts' house, and when the evening wound down, the visitors asked for directions to the yacht club, which was only a quarter mile away. The hosts offered to take them and show them the way in, but the guests declined, saying it was late, too much trouble, and they could find their way easily enough. The hosts gave them the simple street directions, detailed the yacht club's entrance, the ship models, the foyer and the staircase. "The rooms aren't numbered, but just go in the front, up the staircase, and your room is the first door on the right.

The visitors said they would be fine, got in their rental car, and headed for the yacht club. Though they followed directions carefully, they didn't get it *quite* right, and instead entered my boss's house, where everyone was asleep, but the big front porch and foyer were well lit and the front door not locked. Quietly, suitcases in hand, they made their way up the stairs, and opened the door to the first room on the right. It was a nicely made-up guest room, and, like Goldilocks, they fell into a bed that was just right, and had a lovely sleep. In the morning, they made their way downstairs, suitcases in hand, and into the foyer. Looking around, they spied a man (my boss) sitting alone at a large table in a large dining room adjacent to the foyer. His housekeeper, dressed in white, was serving him something.

"Excuse me, is this where we sit to get some breakfast?" the wife of the couple asked, putting down her suitcase.

My boss looked up from his breakfast, cocked his head, studied the two as one might look at a wild new abstract painting, took a sip of his coffee, and said:

"Well, I don't know who you are, or what you're doing in my house, but what the hell, since you're here, you might as well sit down and have some grub."

Somewhat of a Wizard

We met on the wharf during one of those windy, damp early spring days of my 21st year. It was 1971, the year I was getting my boat ready for sea. I did my task of living on my boat those days. I say task because it was; I wasn't happy. I was insecure and uncertain about what I was doing with my life. There seemed no therapy. I strained and worked at even the simplest daily jobs. The only thing I could do easily was read. That was good, anyway. I had my boat and I was going to sail the oceans of the world. I had money. And yet in the morning I'd wake up nauseous and wish the day over and for all I had there was really nothing.

Then I met Snap. He was an elderly gent, and he stood next to a boat somewhat like mine. "Heading to sea?" I asked him. He looked like he was. (You can tell these things when you've been around boats.)

"Hello Hello," he said, adjusting his glasses at me as if they were a monocle. "My name's Snap, and yes, in answer to you, we're headed to England."

"My name's David."

"Pleasure, mine, fully, is Snapenbackprebeckenbottom. Robert Snapenbackprebeckenbottom."

He said it with finesse. Anyone else would have slurred it.

"But please call me Snap," he added with a smile. He was very British, and he seemed weird from the start. But God, he was likable.

"I like your boat," I said, deciding he'd probably heard enough comments about his name.

"Yes, well, Fair Susan and I plan to go first to England, and then I plan to get quite away from things."

"Is Fair Susan your boat's name?" I asked.

Snap chuckled and patted the boom. "No, no dear boy, Fair Susan is my mate, my companion, my confidant, my partner and, indisputably, my wife."

"Oh," I said somewhat embarrassed. "And does your boat have a name?"

"Never sir. Giving a fine craft a human name like Fair Susan would certainly be a desecration in the fullest sense of the word. I would not for one moment think of such a relegation."

"Sounds like you're a bit down on people," I said.

"My friends are inanimate, sir. They are part of me, because I make them myself. And thus they become the best of friends... as honest as I, as predictable as I, because they are me!"

I didn't know what to say. I stood there, oblivious to the damp cold air that whistled around the pilings and boats. Snap headed toward me. For just an instant he seemed to search me with his eyes, as if he wasn't quite sure whether to let me into his life. And then he smiled and said, as if wondering what I was waiting for, "Well come aboard and have some tea and warm up. It's frightful outside."

In the snug cabin he handed me a cup of hot tea. I settled down in a corduroy covered settee, and watched him as he precisely cut bread into small pieces. His eyes gleamed, and he was humming to himself and pulling on his foot long gray beard.

"You deal in contradictions, Snap," I said. I just said it. It slipped out, from the back of my mind, through my lips, and into the air.

He was carefully buttering each piece of bread. "Life is a contradiction, and I am as much a part of it as you or this vessel." He put the pieces of bread on a plate and placed them on the table in front of me.

"A contradiction of what?" I asked.

"Itself, many times. And speaking of contradictions, Fair Susan will be along in a few moments."

"I have trouble picturing what she will look like," I said, surprised at my own candor.

"She's very pretty, and much younger than I, and you'll think, "There's an odd couple. But when you get over your presumptions, you'll find it is not us who are odd at all." He paused and looked down at the bread. Then he looked me hard in the eyes. "What is 'odd' anyway? Who is to judge what is odd and what isn't? And even if we are 'odd' by common definition, being odd is not something from which to shy away."

"I'll be scared to think anything now," I said, smiling.

"Judge us as you would judge yourself, strive to find the real essence, for there is the soul, and from there is where real love and friendship emanate."

He talked as if he were acting in a Shakespearean drama. If he made me nervous, I wouldn't have liked the man. But there was nothing hard pressed about him. He was more mesmerizing than anything else.

Suddenly there was someone else to contemplate. A young woman swung down from the companionway hatch and presented herself abruptly in front of me.

"Why, you've made a new friend, Snap," she said to him, all the time looking at me.

"Fair Susan, may I present David," Snap said, extending his arm toward me in a theatrical manner. I stood, bumping the table and spilling my tea. "God, I'm sorry, " I said.

"Don't apologize to him," Snap said, looking toward heaven. "It's Fair Susan here that is to blame." He gave a pleasant smile. "Indirectly, of course," he added as he reached over to mop up the tea with a sponge.

"I'm pleased to meet you," I said.

"The feeling is mutual, and I hope you'll stay for dinner."

"Well, really, I just met..."

"Of course he will, Fair Susan, he has no one else to dine with," Snap said. He looked over at me kindly. "I trust I'm right, David."

"I guess my social calendar is a bit light today," I said.

"Splendid," Snap said. "Then after we finish tea we'll be on our way."

"On our way?" I asked

"Yes, oh, I guess I forgot to include the fact that we haven't moved aboard as yet, and live in a somewhat oversized estate some twenty miles north of Boston."

"But how will I get back?"

"At eight o'clock on the morrow, as we will," Snap replied. He smiled and finished his tea.

"And now," Snap said," If old Samuel will come to life, we'll whisk off to the castle, Fair Susan's domain."

Samuel was a car. But not just any car. In fact, you'd have your hands full trying to prove to Snap that Samuel wasn't a real live faithful old servant. Samuel was a Rolls Royce, and as tired a Rolls Royce as ever came down the pike.

"Brought him from a fellow podiatrist who was sued for malpractice and lost the case frightfully," Snap said. "Fellow must have handled old Samuel here as he did his patients' feet. Nearly snuffed his life away. He patted the once regal machine. "But I aim to bring him back to his full working capacity," he continued, "and then we'll be lifelong friends." A benevolent smile came to his whiskered face. It was cold and I started to shake. Then the ritual began.

"All right, Samuel, time to head to that heated garage now, and I do apologize for this lot of miserable weather. We can't change it so let's just live with it. Ignition, old fellow." Samuel turned over, but there was no spark of life. Rather than wear down the battery, Snap turned off the key and then shook his head with a smile. He got out, went around to the trunk of the car, removed something, and walked around to the hood. He held something about the size of a grapefruit in his hands, but before I could get a good look, the hood had opened and he'd vanished behind it. The harsh wind whistled around the car, and mixed in with it I thought I heard Snap's voice.

"What's he doing?" I ventured to Fair Susan.

"Snap is somewhat of a wizard," she said, and smiled with admiration.

I got out to look. Snap stood against the radiator, holding what looked like a crystal ball over the engine and mumbling some sort of abracadabra. I decided it was time to go back to my boat and cook some hash; the situation was too absurd for my liking. But before I turned, Snap looked over at me, smiled, and said. "Be a good sport David and turn the engine over."

I got in the car, turned the key, and it started. "It started!" I said, amazed and wide-eyed.

"It does more than it doesn't," Fair Susan said with pride. Snap got in and I slid over, the three of us now in the front seat. We drove away. Snap seemed totally engulfed in pride for Samuel. After a few minutes, I broke the silence.

"How can a foot doctor be sued?" I asked.

"It was quite simple," Snap replied. "He operated on the wrong foot."

After about 15 minutes on the road we started getting into more country-like surroundings. Snap eased Samuel down a winding country road, all the time giving a narration of the histories of this house and that along the way. These were definitely mansions; those that I could see, anyway. Many had driveways so long and winding that only the size of the entrance could suggest the opulence of the house behind.

"Many used to have iron fences around the estate but I hear tell that all that iron was given to the war effort in WWII," Snap said.

"Very patriotic," I said, not really sure whether to sound sarcastic, serious, or humorous.

"Rather capricious and pretty bloody stupid," Snap said with a futile tone. And then his voice lifted, theatrically. "But there are iron gates at this fine estate," he said. And he turned into the driveway.

"Incredible," I said as we approached the house.

"Incredible, but not particularly livable," Snap said with an amused smile. "Kind of like living in a furnished warehouse. We have come to find nothing cozy about giant rooms with thirty foot ceilings." He paused to have a private chuckle with himself. "I have more the court jester in me than the king, and find smaller quarters quite adequate for carrying on the privilege of living."

We went inside through a tall oak door with a giant brass knocker, and walked through a number of rooms, indeed oversized and with tall ceilings. They were full of furniture, but it was covered in white drop clothes. The place did look like a warehouse. I held back my questions as I was led down corridors and through large dusty rooms. We passed the kitchen, more like a restaurant kitchen than house kitchen, with its long stainless counters, and huge black iron stove and oven. Then we went through a door in the back of the house and entered a small two-room apartment.

"This, dear David, is where the court jester and his Fair Susan reside. Shall we relax and have some brandy... blackberry or plain?"

I gave him a preoccupied nod and mumbled something like 'either one'. "You must have just moved in," I blurted.

"No, to the contrary, we've been here about two years," Snap said. He looked toward Fair Susan and so did I. Isn't that about right?" he asked her.

Fair Susan smiled and nodded. I had not seen her without her big Cossack hat and long winter coat. She was in the process of removing it and was arching her back in such a way as to give me a good view of her front. I was hooked on Fair Susan. I liked her deep warm smile, her bright and lively eyes, and now I knew I liked her body. Snap had been watching me look at her.

"I prefer her feet," he said with a smirk.

Blood rushed to and flushed my face. "Then why do you live in this tiny section of the house," I quickly asked, filling a deadly silence I was sure would come.

"Too much to clean," Snap said. "And why should we live like kings when we have always detested royalty?"

"But you bought the place," I said.

"On the contrary, David, Fair Susan here inherited it…lock, stock and chandelier."

"It must be worth a small fortune," I said.

"To some people's way of thinking, I suppose, but to our meaning of the word 'fortune', it is nothing at all," Snap said, handing me a small glass of brandy. And then he continued, "In this small apartment we can stay just as warm, sleep as well, talk as well, keep our faiths as well, think as well, and, despite the ballroom being on the other wing of the house, dance as well." And with that he picked up Fair Susan (although she was much bigger than he) and danced her around the room. In all his exuberance he toppled over a small end table. "Well, almost as well," he added, and laughed and laughed and laughed. He only stopped because he ran out of breath. As soon as he caught his breath, he turned to Fair Susan and asked, "Well, who shall do the cooking and who shall do the entertaining?" But before she could answer he said, "Stroganoff, I'll make my Stroganoff," and he was headed to the refrigerator.

I went to the sofa and sat down. Fair Susan went over to the record player. I watched her as she aimlessly pulled a record out of a thick stack of albums. Snap, his back toward us, was busy pulling things out of the refrigerator. Just as Fair Susan pulled the record of out its jacket, Snap started singing. When she played the record, the first song was the one Snap was singing. I was amazed! But neither of them seemed to notice. I felt like I'd smoked a funny cigarette. I bumbled my awe to Fair Susan. She obviously hadn't noticed, but she smiled with understanding and said, "Oh, that happens so much I don't even notice it sometimes." We both sipped our brandy.

"So you're going to sail the world," I said nervously.

"We certainly wish to, and soon," she said. "But first, we must get a crew together."

"Can't the two of you handle the boat?" I asked.

"We can't sail," she said and smiled.

I managed an "oh" and tried to look pensive, but my mind was blank. Snap seemed to have heard Fair Susan.

"We had a crew lined up you see," he said, "but these Americans are so damn unreliable." He paused and looked at his Stroganoff. "And weird," he added.

That evening we ate the best dinner I'd ever had: beef stroganoff, fresh rolls, buttered asparagus, and a delicious red wine. The first half of the dinner was filled only with my comments about how tasty everything was, and with Snap's humble thanks. Then Snap, chewing on a mouthful, suddenly said, "You know, David, I believe that all bodily ailments can be cured through manipulation of the feet."

I managed another "oh" and tried to look pensive again.

"No, it's true," Snap continued, immediately seeing through my pretense of thought. "You see, the foot is ultimately the final receptor of all bodily activity. And, as that follows, it only follows that through reverse manipulation, that is, from foot to head, any improperly functioning area can be manipulated back into proper working order. Of course, dear David, that is a superficial explanation, to say the least."

"Come on Snap, " I said with a broad smile.

Snap got angry. It was the only time I ever saw him the least bit unlovable. "David," he said, pointing a quivering finger at me, "you obviously have yet to fathom the fact that everything...and I mean EVERYTHING... in this world is connected."

"Yes, but Snap..."

He put his arm around me and looked at me in such a way as to say, 'The subject is closed and the anger is gone.'

There was an eerie silence throughout the rest of dinner and the dishes (which Snap and Fair Susan did, refusing to let me lift a finger). Afterwards, Snap put on some synthesizer music, and poured me a glass of Courvoisier. We drank and listened and talked about music. Then, out of the blue, Snap asked, " David, will you sail to England with us?" There were a dozen reasons why I couldn't accept. "Sure," I said.

That seemed all that was necessary for that night. For Snap, at least. He stood up, stretched, and said, "Well, at the risk of strangling a cliché, tomorrow is indeed another day. If you'll excuse me now, I'm afraid the days get shorter in proportion to one's life, at least after thirty." And he chuckled and patted my shoulder. "Not your problem though, my new friend."

I stood. "Snap, thanks for everything. I'm very glad we met today," I said. Never had I been so sincere.

"David," Snap said formally, "I bid you a good night's sleep." He looked toward his wife. "Fair Susan, you're lucky to be young enough not to poop out in front of our new found friend and guest. Don't stay up too late, however, we've got lots of planning to do in the morning. Good night all."

"May I get you another glass of Courvoisier?" Fair Susan asked after Snap had left the room.

"Sure."

She smiled at me warmly, then got up to re-fill our glasses. At the bar, with her back toward me, she asked, "How can you decide so fast, David?"

"About what?"

She turned toward me. "Going with us on the trip," she said.

"Oh, I don't know. I guess just by instinct."

"What do you mean?"

"It's natural to want to feel wanted. And I felt wanted then, so I accepted."

"Do you think you know us well enough?" she asked. She handed me my glass and sat down near me on the couch.

"I will before we leave. We've got quite a bit of preparing to do."

"No, the boat's ready to go. The canned food is all loaded and marked. There's mostly just cosmetic work left...varnishing and things like that," she said. She moved closer to me and looked straight in my eyes, her face warm and inviting. "I wish we had a nice cozy fire in front of us," she said softly. She took a sip of her drink. "You were lonely, weren't you?" she asked.

"When?"

"Before. Before today."

"I'm starting to think so," I said with a nervous laugh.

"Didn't you know?"

"I thought it was something else," I said. "I thought it was my need to fulfill my dream, which was to sail around the world.

"But it wasn't?"

"Let's just say that I don't think sailing around the world would do the trick," I said.

"No?"

"No," I said.

I smiled and slowly shook my head. For the first time in months, I somehow felt alive, satisfied, and a part of something bigger than myself. I felt there would be no more nauseous mornings.

She looked me in the eyes and moved closer. I felt a drop of sweat slide down my side. I groped for something to say. "Ah, Fair Susan, what *is* your real name?"

"It's Susan," she said. "The Fair" is something Snap came up with quite awhile ago.

"He's a wonderful person," I said. "I've never been influenced so fast by anyone. How did you two meet?"

"It was in Africa, on a safari, about five years ago. We were signed up together on one of those group tour things. It was incredibly hot, so much so that no one was having a good time. They all were doubly mad because they wanted to get their money's worth and the whole ten days was hot as hell. Then there was Snap. The heat seemed to go right through him, and back up into the sultry air. He whisked it aside, and attended to the safari with a great desire to learn. He learned about guns, tracking, animal nature, and a host of other things. The rest of us just sat around and bitched about the heat. With all our might and skills, we devised awnings, fans, and even hung wet towels around us. We tried everything we could to get away from the heat during those ten days. About the third day I asked Snap how he could stand the heat. And he looked at me cheerfully and said, 'You are in the land of heat, you must accept it for what it is, live with it, or leave.' Everything he said after that made sense to me, and he seemed as if he had life in control, and that's what I wanted. I couldn't control my life, my impulses. But he could. I wanted what he had. One thing led to another, and we were married."

"Quite a story," I said. There was a long awkward silence. "Quite a story," I said again, shaking my head self-consciously. She didn't say anything. She only looked at me, with a desirous expression in her eyes. I got nervous again. "Well," I said, "it's been such a good day I better get some sleep before I stay up too late and waste the next one."

She strained to be frivolous. "OK, party-pooper, I'll show you to your quarters."

I smiled and stood up. She got up and I followed her through corridors and up stairways until we reached the room that was to be mine for the night.

"If I have to find the bathroom in the middle of the night I may get lost forever. This place is huge," I said.

"It's right down the hall at the end," she said. "And, David, thanks for coming along when you did. See you in the morning." She squeezed my arm. "Sweet dreams," she said softly.

I didn't look at the clock, but it must have been about two in the morning when the door opened. I smelled perfume and knew who it was. She slid into bed and nuzzled against me, spoon fashion. She was breathing heavily; I could feel her chest move against me. I rolled over, pretending to just awaken. She kissed me eagerly and then we made love. She never took off her nightgown. My heart fluttered, pounded, and then ached. It was all very fast and it was over. Then she took the nightgown off, and we made love again very slowly, and it was love, and I felt love. Neither of us ever said a word. Then she slid out of the bed and the room quietly.

I awoke about nine and got up. The whole thing seemed like a dream, only I could smell her body on my fingers and perfume on the sheets. I lingered in my room until ten, scared to leave and not knowing what to do next. My mind was transfused with feelings of love, passion, guilt and anxiety. Finally, I went downstairs. There was no one. I entered the apartment in the back, found no one in the kitchen-dining room area, and, after some hesitation, I walked down the short hall and knocked on the bedroom door. There was no answer. I opened it a crack and looked in. Fair Susan was asleep alone in the bed.

"Time to wake up," I said.

She rubbed her eyes and then sat up, pushing her long brown hair back over her shoulders.

"Oh good morning," she said.

"Where's Snap?" I asked.

Snap was not on the premises. We looked everywhere. Then we noticed that Samuel was gone. With that Fair Susan said anxiously, "He's down at the wharf. I know he is. We'd better take a cab."

When we arrived at the wharf, Snap's boat was gone. Fair Susan turned to me and said, like a child first confronting reality, "He's left for England. I know it. He's sailing the boat to England."

"But he can't really sail," I said. My face prickled. I felt panic stricken, helpless.

"The boat will take care of him; they're close friends," she said, a strange futile tone to her voice.

We walked to the end of the wharf, not touching, each looking vainly out to sea. At the end we just stood and looked out at nothing for the longest time.

"You told him," I said finally.

"No," she answered.

I believed her somehow, and didn't say anything. A strong breeze blew out of the west.

After a while she continued, "He didn't know, really. But he just senses things. He sensed it I'm sure." Her voice wavered. She started shaking, then convulsed, and broke into deep, thick sobs. "He was all I ever had, and I didn't even know it." She said that, over and over. She leaned on me for physical support, nothing else. I felt lifeless, wooden, like the pilings around me.

We walked back, slowly. I noticed that Samuel was parked near where the boat used to be. We got in the car, out of the wind. I looked and saw that Snap had left the keys in the ignition, and I knew it would be best if we got away from there. I turned the key but Samuel would not start. Helpless, I looked over at Fair Susan. She was rocking slowly, cradling her head in her hands. The west wind blew through the pilings and shook the old car slightly.

BIG RED AND DRIVING
THE BEND

The year I met Big Red I was living alone in an ark under a bridge in St. Paul, Minnesota on the Upper Mississippi River. *Dave's Ark* was a 42-foot home-built steel houseboat which, due to its ancient and long-ago seized-up Ford 302 engines, never went much of anywhere. But that was OK because I spent most of my waking hours running a 135-foot stern wheel cruise ship along the Mississippi and Minnesota Rivers. On the rare Saturday evenings I had off, I would climb over a tired security fence on the shore beside my houseboat, ascend the more than 100 rusty steel stairs that led to the top of the Wabasha Avenue Bridge, walk across the span of the Mississippi, and stand outside the World Theatre with a tall shy man in a white suit. Together, we would try to muster in enough people to generate audience noise for his local radio show. The year was 1978, the show was *A Prairie Home Companion*, and the tall shy man was Garrison Keillor. Later, he got real famous. I didn't. But that's OK, too, because in watching and listening to his mesmerizing monologues I truly learned to appreciate the art of story telling.

After one particular show and after an earlier incident on the river I'll never forget, I walked back across the bridge, but didn't descend the stairs to my houseboat as usual. Instead I continued on to a river bar called Awada's. I was still jittery from what had happened that morning and thought a drink or two might calm me down. At this point I didn't know many of the river pilots, as I was a new transplant from the ocean, and considered just a 'cub pilot'– green, newly licensed and still learning the river. I functioned in a make believe, tourist-focused world, driving a recreated Mississippi River sternwheeler and narrating with authority about a river I knew little about. As a sternwheeler captain, I wore a uniform designed by the cruise ship's marketing department and calculated to radiate authority and a sense of command. It consisted of white boat shoes, blue pressed slacks, a belt with a big brass buckle showcasing a Mississippi sternwheeler, a white shirt with four gold bar epaulets, and a name tag that said 'Captain'. Thank God there was no hat. Believe me, I never wandered too far off the ship in this get-up. And the very last place on earth I would ever go in this rig was the world of Awada's Riverfront Tavern, the domain of the hardscrabble commercial towboat pilots, whose uniforms consisted of what was closest to them on the floor when they got up each morning. Towboats, by the way, actually *push* rather than *tow* barges, and what they and their pilots do is extraordinary. Their emotions on the job fluctuate between complete boredom and total terror. Pushing barges with a million gallons of gasoline through steel bridge spans in a fast running river in the middle of a city in the dark of night is not for the faint of heart, especially when the bow or 'head' of the tow can be a couple of football fields in length ahead of you. In fact, the largest tow ever pushed on the Mississippi is eight barges long by four barges wide. That's makes it a 1600 foot ship with a 200 foot beam on a narrow river. So next time you think you're hot stuff docking your 30 footer with your bow thruster, think again.

So I wandered into the smoke-filled darkness of Awada's in my jeans and tee shirt, took a seat at the bar, and ordered a Grain Belt beer. Before long, four men came in and grabbed a round table just behind my bar seat. I stole a glance at them over my shoulder, but the big one with the red beard caught my eye. "Hey," he said, in a deep, gravelly voice, "I seen you from my pilot house today...can tell it's you there, Cubby, even without yer little Captain America suit. You're that new one runnin' that silly paddle boat that looks like a giant wedding cake, ain't you?" He stopped to wave over the waitress, then continued. "Passed you kinda tight in Monkey Rudder Bend while we was pushing a couple of empties down from Lock 1 this morning. 'Nother few feet and I coulda squished you down through that Mississippi River mud right to China. Mebbe you happened to notice me."

"You're off the *Sadie Mae*," I said. "That's why I'm here drinking. That mud you mention was in my Captain America pants when I came around the bend with my 300 tourists and found you and your 400 feet of barges bearing down on us, taking up most of the river."

"Yeah, I was *drivin'* that bend with them barges there, Cubby. Some guys, they'll *back* a bend instead of drivin' it...let the currents pull their lead barges through while backing slow against it to try to get control." He looked over at the other three pilots at the table, and they all smirked. "'Backin' Jacks'...that's what we call them guys. Backin' Jacks waste time, stretch their tows across the whole river, backin' and trying to line up for the next bend. Them's cub pilots, like you. You got to drive a bend, son. Kind of like a car in a skid. Got to let go the brakes, put the hammer down on them 3000 horses, and steer through it... also maybe hope there ain't nobody around the corner." Red smiled. "Look here Cubby," he continued, "you might as well come over and join us. Might learn a thing or two."

So I grabbed my Grain Belt and moved over and met the pilots of the *Sadie May*, the *Mike Harris*, the *Itaska*, and the *Bull Duram*.

The waitress came by and stood next to Red, who clasped her tiny hand in his mighty paw, and then released into it a one hundred dollar bill. "Sweetie, I want you to fill the top of this round table with open Budweiser bottles 'til you can't see the top no more. Then kindly go away, cause we don't want no interruptin' as we got some cards to play and some stories to tell, and it's been one long day on the river."

Then he looked over at me and winked. "Ain't that right there, Cubby?" he said, and, just light enough not to hurt me, my new friend punched me on the shoulder.

WATCHING VASTNESS

Late afternoon finds her standing at the very edge of the sea, waves just touching her toes, the rising onshore breeze lifting her hair, sunlight glowing against her skin and faded neon bikini. One of the locals, one of the women who brings no accessories to the edge of the world, stares seaward, watching something invisible to the summer people who walk behind her, between her back and the dunes. Now and then some inlander stops to follow her stare, focusing and refocusing on the immensity of waves beyond the surf, then gives up and strolls on, content to look a few yards ahead. Only the other locals know that the woman watches vastness.

So writes John Stilgoe in his book *Alongshore*. It makes me wonder: Why do we watch vastness? We sailors look seaward, yearning, searching, but it's not just because we're sailors. The landsman who lives on the shore does the same. Are we attracted to water because we ourselves are 72 percent water? Or that our earth's surface is *also* 72 percent water? Or do we look out to sea because of our inquiring nature as humans? Do we want something that is 'out there' because it's not 'here'? Why then, when we sailors are finally out on the vast empty sea, do we then look and yearn for land. Perhaps it's all about 'looming'. Herman Melville writes of it early on in *Moby Dick*, how on any Sunday afternoon, there are "thousands upon thousands of mortal men fixed in ocean reveries...some leaning against the spiles; some seated upon the pier heads; some looking over the bulwarks of ships from China...as if striving to get a better seaward peep." Seamen have long known this act of gazing over the horizon as *looming*.

I remember first thinking about this looming business during an offshore delivery from New England waters to the Caribbean, late one fall many years ago. I had a sketchy boat, and an even sketchier crew of three: two questionable characters who needed a cheap ride south for the winter, and a big, tough, red-bearded, ex-Vietnam helicopter pilot turned Mississippi River towboat pilot friend who had never sailed before but thought this was as good a way as any to get a strong dose of it. I told Big Red as tactfully as I could that it would be different out there on the ocean, that shore and society wouldn't be close as it is on the river, that it would be day after day of vast open ocean, and, perhaps, huge waves and storms.

Big Red looked at me, leaned toward me, and cocked his head inquiringly: "I ain't afraid of any of that dying shit, if that's what yer getting at," he said. End of discussion. Anyway, when we got offshore, I noticed how everyone on board, myself included, fell into "looming" mode, especially Big Red, who, despite any land being hundreds of miles off, just kept watching the vastness, looking over the horizon. One hundred miles short of Bermuda, the ocean began to get rough. Then it got rougher. When we went off a particularly large wave, and the combination engine box/table in the center of the cabin lifted up off its mountings, we called it quits and hove to. When it got too scary up on deck, we all went below and lay on the cabin sole, except for Big Red, who squeezed into a port side pilot berth. When we fell off another breaking sea and Big Red was thrown out of the berth and into the cabin table, he sheared off half of one of his front teeth. "Makes me look tough I bet, don't it?" he asked. And when we were completely submerged by a third wave and the cabin interior went quiet and turned Atlantic Ocean green, Big Red started calmly singing Dylan's "Oh, Mama, Can This Really be the End". Obviously, it wasn't. When we finally did get to St. Thomas, I gave Big Red his return air ticket at a thatched-roof bar on a pier end in Charlotte Amalie. He was staring out at the harbor's mouth, lost in thought. I was doing the same. I was thinking of vastness and how, after more than two weeks at sea yearning for land, here we were staring out to sea again. I was thinking about how, as humans, we've been around for a mere 200,000 years, compared to our four billion year old oceans. Our planet's highest mountains were once covered with water; up on Mount Everest, we've found fossils of animals that once lived at the bottom of the sea. Really, I thought, we humans are just highly specialized fish adapted to our 21% land mass. Our limbs came from fins; our jaws from gills. So maybe that's why we still look out to sea, and then look back.

Just then, Red, still looking seaward, interrupted my thoughts.

"How about another Heineken there, Cappy, before you and me dive into them fish tacos?" he asked.

I looked over warmly at my old friend; we'd been through a lot together, and his spirits had never wavered. I wanted to say that to him, but I didn't.

"You know, *you're* really a fish, Red," I said instead.

He scratched his big red beard, and turned to look back at me, his broken front tooth giving him a jack-o-lantern look when he smiled.

"I been called worse," he replied as he threw a big arm around me. And then he lifted his empty green bottle toward the bartender.

TOTO, WE'RE NOT IN KANSAS ANYMORE

It's 3:22 am on a Friday in June and I'm sitting on *Elsa's* starboard berth looking across at a small oil painting of Marblehead Harbor that highlights a handful of gaff-rigged sloops and schooners from another century. The painting has a wonderful patina and now, further illuminated by the gimbaled kerosene lamp near its gold frame, it holds my gaze for more than a few moments. I'm up at 3:22 a.m. because I awoke with an idea for a column I write, and I knew a deadline was fast approaching. No more time for staring at a painting. While my mini laptop is firing up, I flip on the VHF and turn it to 'scan', maybe yearning for some company at this odd hour. My column was going to be about how 99.9 percent of boaters don't know how to dock. Snobbish of me, but true. I begin outlining the physics of why one can quite easily dock, initially, without any bow or stern lines and even without any bow or stern person. It's always bugged me to see the dangerous way that people dock, throwing and missing lines, jumping off the deck too early, cleating bow lines too early and springing the stern out away from the dock, often generating much yelling and scrambling all around, and even perhaps an unplanned swim between dock and boat. When docking the wrong way, things can change for the worse mighty quick.

I was thinking about all this when the VHF stopped scanning and started blaring its emergency signal on Channel 16. About the same time I heard a few raindrops on the cabin top which sounded oddly heavy, like falling fishing weights. *Tornado watch; possible two-inch hail stones, and 70-knot winds possible*, the digitized man on the VHF told me. So I forgot about my docking column and got to thinking about tornados, which seemed appropriate given the moment. Besides, rowing ashore right then seemed a bad idea.

A couple of summers ago I was headed alone from Marblehead to Maine on *Elsa*. At the eastern end of the Annisquam Canal, which bisects Cape Ann, I began to head back out to sea for the 20-mile stretch to the Isles of Shoals off the New Hampshire coast, when the sky sent a poignant message. About the same time my low end (read: not smart) cell phone rang. It was my gadget head, weather head friend. "Stay in the Annisquam," he commanded, "I'm tracking these death cells and even a tornado on my iPhone, and you'll get hit for sure before you make Isle of Shoals." "Thanks," I said. "I will, but keep me posted, ok? And, by the way, do you always have to call them 'death cells'? How about just saying 'bad thunderstorms'?"

"You know David, if you weren't so cheap and had a smart phone yourself, you'd see what I mean." Then he hung up his really smart phone, no doubt moving on to another 'app', (maybe one predicting 21st century atmospheric anomalies off the Isles of Shoals), and left me waiting. The next morning at dawn he called me again. "Go go go…go right now. Go go go. I've computed a window of under five hours for you to make it to the Shoals between death cells if you leave right now." So off I went, pushing *Elsa* for all she was worth, while looking over my shoulder for the rapidly encroaching death cells. After my arrival at a safe mooring, the sky fell, the death cells came, and tornados hit New Hampshire. One person was killed.

Before this the closest I had ever come to a tornado was on the Mississippi River in St. Paul one summer. I was captaining a stern-wheel-driven river cruise ship at the time, and on this particular trip we were loaded with a band, dinner, a giant wedding cake, one groom, one bride, 400 guests, a gaggle of caterers, and my crew of five. I was particularly excited about this charter because I love wedding cake and as captain I was certain I could score a big piece. As we headed upstream along the heavily-wooded, state park section of the river, I received a vhf warning about a tornado heading east toward Minneapolis and St. Paul. On the intercom I called my crew chief, who was two decks below managing a very busy bar. I could hear the band in the background blaring "Rollin on the River" for what must have been the hundredth time this summer.

"Shawn, I need you in the pilot house RIGHT NOW," I said. Shawn was a sincere, fairly innocent 21-year-old college senior who had been my crew chief for three summers. It seemed I'd just turned off the intercom when, bingo, there he was, breathing heavily but standing proudly at the door in his white shirt with its two gold epaulets. "Hey, Cap, what's up?"

"Tornado coming very soon, Chief. I'm taking all 135 feet of this floating wedding cake and driving her into the trees, then holding her there tight with the engaged paddlewheel. I want you to get another crewman on the winch, drop the swing stage ramp over the bow, and when the bow hits the beach, grab your heaviest anchor line, jump ashore off the stage, and tie it to the biggest tree you can find. Then I want you to have the crew close all the windows on the main deck. And do it *subtly* Shawn. I don't want the guests to know about the tornado until they have to. I don't want panic. If it's going to hit us for sure, I'll announce over the P.A. for everyone to move to the main deck; you and the whole crew will then get every single person to do so. Just say, 'Captain's orders' if they ask why. I don't want panicked people jumping into the water or running into the woods."

Shawn took in all the information with utter concern, his eyes darting from me to the sky in the west.

"And Chief," I added, "When you're done with tying off, come back to the pilothouse."

And off he went. Even though she's 135 feet long, this sternwheeler was flat-bottomed and drew only two feet of water, making a beachable ship! All went well and Shawn dutifully returned to the pilot house. "Put on a lifejacket," I said as he entered. "It's headed this way. Got reports that giant elms to the west of Minneapolis have been yanked from their roots, six foot pieces of the sidewalk still attached." Shawn sat in the corner of the pilothouse, stared at the sky, hands folded tightly in his lap, and slowly turned as white as a Minnesotan in January. I was talking to police, coast guard, and tow boat pilots as the tornado approached. My veteran tow boat pilot friend Big Red, captain of the massively powered *Mike Harris*, was on the radio as usual, following everything. "Better get them two folks married right quick before she hits there, Cappy," he chimed in. "Might be a short marriage, maybe shorter even than some of mine, but that way them two can at least get to heaven together, married and legal and all." Shawn listened to all this very carefully. Then he stood up and walked back and forth, faster and faster, in the pilot house, looking skyward from each side. Finally, he turned to me, his white face seemingly sprouting from his bulky bright orange life jacket. "Cap, please...I'm really scared...Do I have to stay up here?"

Just then the report came in; the tornado had veered north after hitting south Minneapolis, and was tracking away from our Mississippi River location. I watched the color return to Shawn's face.

"Chief," I said, "New assignment for you: go to the main deck and steal me a giant piece of wedding cake."

"My honor, Cap," he said, already heading out the door.

"And Shawn, take off that life jacket. You'll scare somebody."

III

ADULTHOOD

WATCHING THE NEST

The wing of sail divides wind and then wind joins it together again.
Nothing is used, so nothing is wasted.
The Tao of Sailing

Hold those words and bear with me. Think about cycles — life cycles. I know I was, as I sat under *Elsa's* furled mainsail and looked up at the osprey nest above us, crafted into the pines and cedars of magical Quahog Bay. We were all alone, my daughter Alli and I, anchored under this great nest of small branches and twigs. It had been a good trip east from Marblehead over the past few days, and now the weather had deteriorated. But Alli and I were happy here, in one of our favorite spots. There were no other cruising boats and no distractions. It was just us and the osprey nest. And so began a kind of vigil, or I guess a co-vigil, involving both us and the osprey parents. Day and night we listened to their peep, peep, peep, and watched the mother or father leave the nest to scan for predators and search the abundant waters around us for prey to feed to their young one.

"They never both leave the nest at once, Dad. Did you notice that? One always stays back and stands guard, always looking around," Alli said.

"That's their role, sweetie. That's why they exist: to get that chick of theirs big enough to someday fly away and then have a chick of its own."

She thought for awhile.

"Why?"

"Why what?"

"Why go through all that just so you can then be a grown up and then sit there your whole life and watch for predators all over again? Seems like a pain. What's the point."

Hmmm.

I began to think about our family and the last couple of weeks. Our son Nick had had a tough surgery and, though he was twenty-four, my wife watched over him like a hawk (or osprey) over a chick. Her constant vigilance was remarkable. Or maybe not. She would make sure he survived, even if that meant almost 24/7 vigilance, because that was her role. Mother osprey in action. Though it was more than a week after he had come home after surgery, I still felt guilty leaving on the boat and so delayed our departure another day. My wife insisted we go. After all, my business was closed for vacation, Alli had taken time off from her waitress job, and the weather was right. So we cast off.

Life's biggest nightmare is the loss of a child. To me, the nightmare of that nightmare would be having it happen at sea, under my command, so to speak. So I equipped Alli with a whistle around her neck, a brand new submersible hand-held radio clipped to her belt and set on Channel 16, and a harness. I wasn't taking any chances. Still, I suspect the longest time in three days she was alone on deck out of my sight was three minutes. Father osprey in action.

Life moved on. Nick recovered and went back to work. And Alli had to return to work, so she said goodbye to the osprey family. We motored *Elsa* into the always welcoming Great Island Boat Yard at the head of the bay for crew change. Alli's friend Brad drove up for her, and my wife, Mary Kay, arrived by car that evening. Out we went again to the spot under the osprey nest, and Mary Kay took over Alli's observation of the ospreys. The weather stayed nasty, so we stayed put. My wife, like Alli before her, was content just to be there, anchored under the cedars and pines, watching the ospreys.

Sadly, when the weather finally did clear, it was time for her to go back by car, while I awaited still more new crew in a couple of days. Though the boat would seem empty at first, I knew I would have company in the trees above me, and I looked forward to some solo time for thinking and writing.

"I know you love to be alone at times, but why don't you drive home with me for a couple of days, see how Nick is feeling, and then come back with your crew?" Mary Kay asked. It was not a pressurized question, just a thoughtful suggestion. I was torn. And then the cell phone rang. It was Alli.

She was scared. "Dad, I'm broken down in a tow zone in Boston. The brakes went out on the car. I called AAA, but they need to talk to you."

Then the cell phone range again. It was Nick.

"Hey, Dad, are you coming home with Mom?"

"Ah, no, pal. Staying out another week."

Long pause.

"Oh."

"That OK?" I asked.

"Yeah, sure. I guess. I do have two tickets to tomorrow night's Red Sox game and the Jim Rice Hall of Fame ceremony, so I thought..."

There was no longer any hesitation in my mind after those two phone calls.

"We'll be home tomorrow morning," I said.

I felt at peace with the decision to leave, poured a glass of wine for my wife and myself, and settled into my favorite corner of the cockpit. It was then that the sound came. It was the primal sound I've heard only twice before in my life, both times from people experiencing the horrific. But this was not from humans. It was from two ospreys. Somehow, vigilance had been relaxed for just one moment, and the eagle had struck. I looked above to see the pieces of nest and the chick in the big bird's talons, as the frantic osprey parents screamed and then circled the now-empty nest for the next fifteen minutes.

The cycle of life will go on here. I knew there would be more baby ospreys, more osprey parents, more eagles, and more fish spawning around us to feed the cycle. And our life had to move on too; it was time to go. So I raised *Elsa's* well worn mainsail in the gently lifting southwest breeze, and watched silently as the wing of sail divided the wind and then joined it together again.

The Gulf, Golf and the Kid

From the time he was nine years old, and for the next four years, my son Nick and I happily voyaged together along the coast of Maine in our tiny 25 foot sloop. But then, when he turned 13, something happened. He lost interest. I was faced with a challenge. How could I get my now teenaged son to keep cruising in Maine with me, to share in the joy of quiet nights under a blanket of stars, to be away from his friends, away from the activity and noise of youth, away from chicken fingers, away from girls?

Teenagers are a lot like golf balls. You can apply the utmost effort, concentration, training and commitment to getting them to go in the right direction, yet how they act and where they land is often a surprise if not a shock. Like voyaging to the Antarctic, getting ready for a voyage to Maine one-on-one with Nick required forethought and preparation. I needed clearances and permissions. From him. From his mother. I needed to know my opposition and anticipate any number of mental crises. But most importantly, I needed to get him to *want* to go. I needed to bribe him. My son loves golf. It is perhaps the only thing he loves which is not endemic to teenagers. I had my bribe. But his father is a sailor, not a golfer. I went aboard my parents' cruising sailboat in a basket and never looked back. The sea is in my blood, not golf.

And golfers and sailors rarely steer the same course. But I had an idea. "Care for a merger?" I asked my son one day as he sat on his bed watching the walls of his room pulsate to the sound of Puff Daddy on full base.

"What? Speak up!'

"Care for a merger?" I boomed.

Nick looked puzzled.

"A merger," I boomed again. "Could you please lower that... that sound for a moment?"

"What the hell's a merger?"

"We combine our interests... and you don't need to swear."

"What interests?"

"Golf and sailboat cruising. We'll go on a golf cruise on the *Chang Ho*. We'll cruise along the coast of Maine, living on the boat and sailing from golf course to golf course, just the two of us."

I thought I heard him utter the world "cool" but over Puff Daddy and lack of direct eye contact, I couldn't be sure.

"You like that idea Pal?" I ventured hopefully.

Without looking up he said "Dad, chill. I said 'cool' OK?"

I slowly backed out of the room. In my recent studies of teenagers I had learned one thing for certain: if you get an inch, take an inch. There are no miles.

I began to prepare early. First, I knew we'd need to understand one another, my teenager and I. To communicate at all, I discovered would require that I learn a new language — his. This would be my mission prior to departure. So I listened to Puff Daddy, studied teen-age styles of dress, including grunge, and learned what it means and why it evolved. I forced myself to look coldly at a full moon on a warm summer's night, clouds scudding past its face, thinking of it not as the inspirational beauty of nature, but just some big white glob in the sky with some clouds going past. I tried not reading, instead attempting to glean an education and knowledge from television, pop radio and video games. And I tried golf.

Over time I became more and more anxious that my son's interest in the golf cruise would fade, that teen exigencies would eclipse this father-son opportunity. But then one day weeks later, when Nick mentioned that he'd figured a way to mount our golf clubs in the cramped forward cabin of our 25-foot Cape Dory sloop, I knew this cruise was going to happen. I asked Nick to research the harbors that were within walking distance of golf courses.

"Already done," he said confidently, and he showed me his book of public golf courses in Maine. He'd dog-eared the pages with Sebasco, Boothbay, Deer Isle, Rockland and Castine. I nodded, taking an inch and backing out of his room.

" Dad," he said, just as I was closing his door, "what will we do the rest of the time? You know, all the time at sea and at anchor and stuff; you know, when we're not playing golf."

I thought for a minute. I thought of all the reasons we could be harbor bound: fog, pouring rain, high winds. I thought of the 75 square feet of cabin space in the *Chang Ho;* I thought of our inability to communicate and our nearly total lack of common ground. And I suppressed the beginnings of a panic attack.

"We'll bond," I said, and quickly shut his door.

"What if he falls overboard?" my wife asked with great concern, after I'd told her of my plan. "What if he falls overboard and it's in that...that "thick black dungeon fog stuff you're always talking about?"

She had a point. I pictured my son, a black dot disappearing in the grainy mist, yelling, "Dad, Dad, help me. Please." (Well, I thought, at least he's saying "please"). I pictured myself in a growing frenzy, searching blindly, listening, turning the boat left and then right and ultimately in circles all the while screaming his name.

"He won't fall overboard," I said to my wife with authority. "Besides, he doesn't even like to come out of the cabin. He likes it down there with his Discman and Gameboy."

My 12 year-old daughter Alli looked up from her pre-teen magazine. "Well, I think I'll just stay right here thank you very much....maybe do some shopping," she said.

"Oh, and you think those malls of yours are safer places?" I asked.

"At least you can't fall off of one."

"I get the message: You don't want to come along; you don't want to spend two weeks living in *Chang Ho's* cabin with your big brother," I said.

"Dad," she said, with hands on her hips and a burgeoning smirk, "I'd rather wear knee socks, carry an umbrella, and eat Brussels sprouts."

The big day of departure finally arrived. The golf clubs fit just fine up in the bow. My hand-me-down set of antiques, including "Old Rusty" and "The Baffler," went on the bottom, cushioning Nick's shiny new set of top-notch irons. I stowed Nick's sustenance — barbecue chips, Sprite and other nutritious teen-age culinary delights — into the lockers.

My wife and daughter stood on the dock waving goodbye as we headed east in search of the first nine holes of father/son bonding.

"Did Mom yell something?" I asked Nick as we headed out of Salem Harbor.

"I couldn't hear, Dad. But it would be about brushing my teeth. It's always the last thing she says."

Once underway, the cruising routine quickly became clear: Nick would sleep, listen to his music or play Gameboy; I would steer, navigate, adjust sails, cook and do the boat maintenance. It was during that first night out, anchored behind Smuttynose Island at the Isle of Shoals, that I learned Teen-age Lesson #1: *They are nocturnal creatures; it is in the wee hours when they really come alive.* I found that out this first night when I awoke at 3:30 a.m. to the word "cool." He was looking out the porthole over his bunk. "Are we dragging?" I asked, sitting up quickly, "No, wind's up Dad, we should get going. Sailing at night would be cool." So, even though I'd had only four and a half hours of sleep, at 4 a.m. we were underway. At 4:30, two miles out from the harbor, Nick was sound asleep. So much for cool teen-age night sailing. But we had 10 knots of breeze on the quarter; the boat was on automatic pilot and it was bliss.

A couple hours after dawn, I began cooking pancakes. I tried to wake Nick at about 8, and this is when I learned Teen-age Lesson

#2. During the first half of any given day they are varsity sleepers; they will sleep through most any cataclysmic event short of Armageddon (which hasn't yet been tested); they can put Rip Can Winkle to shame. So I ate all the pancakes alone.

The first golf port on our cruise was Sebasco Harbor in eastern Casco Bay. Easy to enter, the harbor is protected in every direction except from the southwest. The very hospitable Sebasco Harbor Resort on the eastern shore has reasonably priced guest moorings, which include launch service and showers. Or, if you're a cheap Yankee like me, you can anchor out. The nine hole course is fun and scenic (and very reasonably priced), with the second hole requiring a shot over a tidal inlet (my ball is the one with a red dot if you find it in the mud at low tide). Nick's score: 39; Dad's score: well, higher (hint to sailors/non-golfers; high in golf is not good). Nick's Sesbasco Harbor Resort chicken fingers rating: 8.25 out of 10. There were no cribbage tournament games that night because Nick discovered an old-fashioned three-lane candlepin bowling alley on the Sebasco property. We played until closing (I lost) and then rowed out in the fog to *Chang Ho's* cozy cabin. The fog cleared that night but the wind came up strong from the southwest. We had a rolly night, but we were warm and dry.

The next day, NOAA weather radio called for "high wave" warnings, with wind and seas from the southwest. I figured if I could just make the five miles to get around Cape Small, it would be a wonderful downhill sleigh ride after that, all the way to Christmas Cove. Nick's job, of course, was to sleep through it, despite the carnival-like ride. Though the *Chang Ho* is by no means remarkable to windward under sail, she's awesome under power, thanks to her narrow, low profile hull and full keel, all pushed by a high-thrust, 4-stroke Yamaha with a three-bladed propeller. (Sure, it's wet, but that's what dodgers are for.) Once around Cape Small, I eagerly rolled out the jib and raised a reefed main. *Chang Ho* took off. The quartering seas were mesmerizing.

As we slid past Seguin Island Light and on toward Damariscove Island, I happily watched *Chang Ho's* stern lift to each sea; then I anxiously watched our dinghy surf toward us on its own wave, falling just short of our transom. At first, it was entertaining; then, as the seas continued to build, I became a bit anxious, though the boat seemed to be doing just fine. A few minutes later, glancing over my shoulder, I saw double trouble, one of those waves upon a wave. The bottom half got under the boat's starboard quarter and lifted us up on our beam ends, while the top one hit the hull full force above the water line. The result was like dropping a shingle sideways into a bathtub; until buoyancy took over we were headed toward China. The port cockpit coaming and part of the dodger went under, but in a few moments we were right back on course. Only the captain was the worse for wear. It wasn't Armageddon, but Rip Van Winkle did awaken. "Dad," Nick said, headphones ajar, "did my basketball shoes get wet?" It was here that I leaned Teen-age Lesson #3: *They fear nothing from Mother Nature because mothers don't scare them.*

We spent the night in Christmas Cove and went ashore for dinner. (Dad needed to chill out.) Nick's chicken fingers rating 8.2. Father/son cribbage tournament after dinner: Nick 3; Dad 0. Required summer reading pages completed 42 (*Cat's Cradle*). Profound dialogue meter score: 0.

After a stop for the night at lovely Harbor Island in Muscongus Bay, we sailed east into West Penobscot Bay on a comfortable broad reach into Rockport. That night, Nick and I walked to Camden for dinner at Cappy's, passing a herd of Belted Galloway cattle on the way. We also detoured by some of the biggest new homes we'd even seen.

"Are they hotels, Dad?" Nick asked.

"No," I said. "They're private homes. They're owned by some executives who work for a big credit card bank."

"How can those people afford such big houses, Dad?"

I pulled out my wallet and handed him my credit card. " See this? " I said.

He studied it. " Yeah?"

"Well, this is one of those things to watch out for in life," I said.

"You mean like fast women?"

"Kind of."

At Cappy's, Nick found top-rated teenager food and root beer; then, after a walk around the busy waterfront, we called a cab to take us back to Rockport and the *Chang Ho*.

Delightful stops over the next few days included the Benjamin River off of Eggemogin Reach and a visit to Woodenboat Magazine's headquarters in Brooklin. Then it was time for our next golf course, so we sailed back through the Reach, rounded Cape Rosier and motored into Castine Harbor. Castine is a great stop, easy to enter with options to either rent a mooring off the Castine Yacht Club or anchor out in wooded Smith Cove across from the harbor. We opted for a mooring close to the yacht club due to our golf plans and soon became the center of attention when we emerged from the tiny cabin with full golf apparel (Nick done up 100% a la Tiger Woods) and two sets of clubs. We gingerly loaded our gear and ourselves into our 7'6" dinghy. The focus stayed on us ashore as we began walking down the street, clubs over our shoulders, full golf attire, and no golf course in sight. That's when the inevitable witticisms from passersby began: "Long par 5, I guess, huh?" (hah hah) and "You guys must have a wicked slice; the course is one mile that way." (hah hah).

Castine is a charming town full of history, great inns, and attractive colonial homes. It also has a pretty 9-hole course with views of the Bagaduce River. And the course really isn't too far from the waterfront. Nick's score: 41; Dad's score: higher. Chicken finger rating at local Castine greasy spoon: 8.8. Father/son cribbage tournament score after dinner: Nick 7; Dad 0. Additional summer reading pages completed: 11 (*Cat's Cradle*). Profound dialogue meter score: still 0.

After a night of relative seclusion in quiet Smith Cove, we headed for our ultimate challenge: a beautiful, top rated 18-hole course in Rockport called Samoset.

"I'm going to bring that course to its knees," I said confidently to Nick on the way across Penobscot Bay. He rolled his eyes.

"Dad, you've never even played an 18-hole course, and never a course with a slope like this."

"Well," I said, " I hope its sloped in my favor."

"Dad," Nick said, exasperated, "slope is a complex formula arrived at from...oh, never mind. Just don't fly the greens; you'll end up in the water."

A little-known secret is that Samoset Resort maintains several guest moorings and a float right off the breakwater close to the property. The cost (free) was right up my alley (but they get even with the green fees). We met my brother Skip, who'd driven up to join us for our final course. Samoset brought us all to our knees. But it sure was pretty and it sure was fun.

Skip would be driving Nick back home to stay with his aunt and uncle while my wife Mary Kay joined me to continue our cruise the next day. Just before bed on Nick's last night aboard, I asked him what he'd learned about his old man after two weeks together in such a small place. I held my breath, hoping for a jump in the pro-found dialogue meter. He thought for a few moments (a good sign). Then, rubbing his chin, he said. "You sure drink a lot of hazelnut coffee." I smiled, resigned to taking an inch where I could, feeling that at least this constituted some form of dialogue.

But then, the next day as he climbed into Skip's van, Nick quickly slipped me a tightly folded piece of paper:

"What's this?" I asked.

"Read it later, Dad. See ya," Nick said. And he was gone.

On the way back to the boat, I carefully unfolded the paper. It was the list of courses he'd planned for next year's golf cruise. That was when I learned Teen-age Lesson #4: *They CAN bond; they'll just be* _real_ *subtle about it.*

ONE ORDER OF PARADISE TO GO

Years ago, back in my boat delivery days, a couple of romantic dreamers hired me to help them on the first leg of their dream: sailing around the world. They were an anxious pair, long on their romantic vision of escaping to sea, but short on the practical part: sailing. That didn't stop them, though. They were excellent at severing ties: they had sold their house, sold both their cars, quit both their jobs, and cancelled their marina slip. They had read all the escapist literature, and even poked out on the bay a few times, but never too far from shore. Nervous about the first leg, they had hired me at the last minute. Forty miles out, on the way to Norfolk, it got rough and unpleasant, the wind brisk and astern. The following seas eyed their vessel hungrily. Strange creaks and groans began to emit from both the vessel and its owners. The missus came up to the cockpit, looked around frantically, and shrieked, "Where's the land? Oh my God. Where the hell is the goddamn land." Anyway, that's another story, but the short version is I was told to "turn around and take us home". So we motored upwind into steep seas for eleven hours, back to the marina where we had started. The owner sat next to me in the cockpit, looking aft and downwind at his vanishing dream. He never let go his grip on the big cockpit cleat beside him. He said nothing. He didn't have to; his white knuckles said it all. In less than one twenty-four hour day, the dream was over.

Robert Pirsig, author of the 1974 best seller, *Zen and the Art of Motorcycle Maintenance*, bought an offshore sailboat with some of the profits from his book, and headed for "The Dream". Years later, he wrote an essay about it in which he said that all that really happens when one 'escapes' the realities of life ashore is simply the substitution of one set of shore-based problems for a new set of ocean-based problems. There is no real escape of problems, pain, pressure, discomfort and worry, only a different set of each, he said. If you understand that, that's fine. If you understand that you don't leave your soul or your past behind when you sail away, that they go everywhere with you, that's fine. Otherwise, to quote Persig: "All this is just running away from reality. You never realize how good that friendly old nine-to-five job can be. Just little things — like everyone saying hello each morning or the supervisor stopping by to get your opinion because he really needs it. And seeing old friends and familiar neighbors and streets you've lived near all your life. Who wants to escape all that? Perhaps what cruising teaches more than anything else is an appreciation of the real world you might otherwise think of as oppressive."

In 1980, when I captained a cruise ship on the Mississippi River in St. Paul, I had a friend who owned a barge company. He'd built it up from scratch into a successful business over many years, but he'd always talked of 'getting out of here', building his dream boat, heading down the Mississippi and then to the Caribbean. Finally, he did it. He sold his company and left. Six weeks later he was back. "The islands all started looking the same," he said. "I'd get up, worry about the anchorage, worry about where I would get water, worry about the next front coming through, and then worry about my next destination, which I wasn't even particularly interested in going to anyway. One island started to look like the last one. I needed some sort of goal. After a while, the goals I did have began to seem empty. I missed my business and all its challenges." My friend sold his boat, came home and bought back his company.

Tristan Jones, who wrote numerous books of his picaresque life sailing the oceans of the world in low budget boats, grew weary of his nomadic lifestyle also. Toward the end of his life he discussed his thoughts about "the dream" and "paradise". Why, he wondered, was turquoise water and an endless white sand beach considered "paradise"? What do you get with paradise, anyway? Challenge? Nourishment? Intrigue? If you anchored off it or sat on it for, say, several days, wouldn't 'paradise' be eclipsed by boredom? Wouldn't it then be time to "escape" paradise?

Well, he's almost convinced me. But maybe I'll give it just one try and see for sure.

I'll see you by that fourth sand dune with the palm tree. Bring the brie; I've got the wine.

SASHA, TASHA AND THE REALITY
OF ROMANCE

The delivery was not one I particularly wanted to make. It was later in the year, probably too late. It was getting too cold to sail south from Rhode Island, and I don't like cold weather at sea. Things freeze and break. People freeze and break. The exposure scares me. The cold numbs my judgment. I make mistakes.

I don't like crossing the New York shipping lanes at night. Or anytime for that matter. Shipping traffic scares me. A leviathan like an LNG tanker hitting a 45-foot sailboat is like a 45-foot sailboat hitting a Styrofoam cup: There's an imperceptible squish and that's it. If I'm squished, I at least want it to be heard.

I don't like 45-foot sailboats that are built like Styrofoam cups; they only bend so far and then they break. Boats that break easily at sea scare me.

I don't like delivering a boat with the owner on board. It almost always leads to complications. Like who's captain. Being hired to be the captain and then not being treated that way bothers me. Then there is a morale-at-sea problem. That scares me.

I don't like sailing shorthanded. When I'm sailing shorthanded I become tired and my mind becomes fuzzy. I make mistakes. I may reduce sail too late, or wrongly plot my position, or do any number of things that endanger the crew and the vessel. I might even die. Dying scares me.

So there were numerous reasons not to take this particular delivery, which was shorthanded, late in the year, with the owner, on a bad boat, going through the shipping lanes, with mixed authority at the helm.

But then again, how bad could it really be?

"He's a novice, but he's a good guy," insisted Clarko, the broker setting up the delivery. "Wife's a little green, too, but what the hell."

"And the boat?"

"Oh, she's an early vintage. You know, back when they used thick fiberglass."

"Clarko, what *is* she?"

"OK, she's a DreamAway 45."

"I'm not going."

"Come on. It's just down to Norfolk, Virginia. Piece of cake. I'd go myself if...."

"Yeah right! Look, it just doesn't sound — how can I put it? — safe. No, my mind's made up."

"He'll pay two hundred a day. Cash."

On Tuesday, I arrived at the marina to find a robin's-egg blue, extremely high-sided sloop sitting at the float. Atop the high sides was a very high cabin, with very large windows — the size you'd find on a Cadillac Eldorado. On top of the cabin, increasing the now seven-foot elevation by two more feet, was the very first powerboat windshield I'd ever seen on a sailboat. Somehow, the whole rig — the boat, cabin, windshield, seemed precariously balanced, as if a sudden sneeze or shout might cause an instant capsize.

High above me in the cockpit sat two grown people and what appeared to be either two large rodents or two very small dogs. The two people seemed out of place, disoriented and nervous, as if they'd been plunked down there by some alien force and told to sit in this strange robin's-egg blue structure and just wait for the end. The dogs — they were dogs, I deduced, because rats rarely wore pink bows in their hair — began yipping incessantly at me.

I approached tentatively, craned my neck and shouted skyward. "Hello up there!" Then I introduced myself and was waved on board. But getting aboard soon became the first leg of the delivery. There was no ladder, so I stopped and pondered my next move, but the owner soon accommodated me by lowering an aluminum gangplank.

He was a slim, dark-haired man who moved about the vessel tentatively, without ease, a stranger in a strange land. " Dean Moloni," he said, extending his hand. His voice had a nervous quiver to it. "And this is my wife Marjorie, " he continued.

Marjorie, who sat huddled in the corner of the cockpit, looked me over disdainfully, the way one might appraise a seemingly untrainable dog. She wore heavy makeup, a short skirt and a pair of plastic disco boots. Honest.

"So.... well, here she is then," I said, after a long uncomfortable pause. I looked up and down the deck. My eyes stopped on the wraparound windshield. "Gee, even got a windshield," I said. " How about that."

"Yup, she's ready to go," Dean said, turning to Marjorie with a slight half hearted nod. There was another long pause. "Be nice and dry up here too, if we ever get a blow," he said, finally. "Want to take a look below?" We went below. I mean *below*. The boat went down and down and down. I looked around. It looked more like a family rec room than a sailing vessel about to head offshore. There were freestanding plants, freestanding chairs, freestanding books and even a freestanding TV. There were large house lamps with plastic still wrapped over the shades. A Hoover upright vacuum stood freely near a frail-looking veneered bulkhead. There was deep-blue shag carpeting everywhere.

Slowly, like gradually rising tide, the realization that a profound mistake was about to happen leaked into my mind. We were headed offshore shorthanded, late in the year, with the owner, on a bad boat, through the shipping lanes.

And we were doing it on a marine Winnebago.

Sasha, one the dogs, broke this thought by nearly breaking the skin on my ankle with her sharp teeth. I reached down toward her tiny canine throat — it seemed a good place to start — but her beady eyes met mine and her teeth clamped harder as I reached toward her. It was as if she were saying, "Go ahead, your foot for my life." Finally, in an unhurried and almost obliging fashion, Marjorie extricated the tiny creature from the skin of my ankle. I was relieved, but made a mental note to arrange another meeting between Sasha and my foot on the lee rail the first dark night offshore. Marjorie tucked the dog into her pink fur-lined ski parka, the dog's ribboned head sticking out under Marjorie's chin. I swear I saw a tiny tongue stick out at me.

Tasha, Sasha's evil twin, was not to be outdone. I first detected her assault by the noise of her claws which made rapid scratching sounds as she raced toward me along the galley countertop. I looked up just in time. In projectile form, Tasha was airborne toward her target: my face. Perhaps she'd defaced other, slower intruders with this method in the past, but what she hadn't counted on was the elbow reflex of an ex-lacrosse goalie. My body turned and my left elbow sprang outward at the projectile. It was not an LNG tanker hitting a Styrofoam cup, but it was close. And it was a clear case of self -defense. Tasha crumbled and landed, like a discarded fur muff, by Marjorie's feet. Marjorie gathered Tasha into her coat, stuffing her next to her sister, and all went aft into the owner's cabin.

Dean looked down and scuffed the toe of one of his new Topsiders along the base of a bunk rail. "The dogs are kind of territorial... sorry," he said, finally.

"Clarko said two hundred a day. That right? " I asked.

"Two hundred a day," he said.

"Two hundred a day and the dogs stay away."

"Two hundred a day and the dogs stay away," he agreed.

Dean showed me around the boat. After asking several technical questions I soon learned the extent of Dean's sailing knowledge. He was what was called an armchair sailor. A romantic couch potato. He'd read all the books, but apparently only focused on the romantic parts. The sailors' references to saltwater sores, endless shivering, hollow eyes from fear and exhaustion — these facts were all eclipsed by the stories of palm tress in Morea and beaches in the Caribbean. When I asked him what sailing he'd done, he merely said, "Around the bay." Then he added, "Usually, Marjorie wants to come in when the sky doesn't look right or the wind begins to pick up. So we never have gotten too far. That's why we need you. Just to check us out over our first leg to Norfolk."

I began to make a list of what was really unsafe, poorly equipped or just plain dangerous on board. Finally I gave up and threw the list away. What they needed was a whole new boat and crew. But what I needed was two hundred a day, and so, at about 9 p.m. I just went to bed in the bow, as far from the malevolent rodent-canines as I could. I had a feeling I'd need the rest. The reality of romance would begin soon enough.

The sound of loud knocking awoke me. It was a knocking against the hull next to my head. There were also voices. Reluctantly, I rose. Working my way aft through the main salon, I encountered Dean. He, too, was headed for the companionway to see what his noise was all about. What we encountered were relatives. Dean and Marjorie's relatives. Lots of Dean and Marjorie's relatives. They bore gifts. In their hands were boxes of donuts. Lots of greasy donuts. Donuts are to going offshore what a match is to gasoline. Donuts are little round time bombs, ready to explode with the least amount of motion. The relatives, like swarming ants, climbed — and I mean climbed — aboard. They were there to say farewell to the valiant voyaging sailors. I moved aside as they clambered aboard. I listened and watched as they chattered and munched donuts. Dean looked uneasy. Marjorie chatted away at a hundred miles an hour. She answered the questions that she could (How do you cook? Where do you sleep?), and she deferred to Dean for those she couldn't (Will you anchor at sea each night)?

Finally, it was over. The donuts were gone. The relatives lowered themselves ashore. It was time to go.

Dean seemed nervous in the face of the relatives and asked me to take *Robin's Egg* (I forget her real name) away from the slip in the marina. As Marjorie secured things below, we cast off and I backed her away from a marina slip that had expired that day. I backed her away from a life onshore, for Dean and Marjorie had sold their home and most of their possessions. I backed her into the future, a romantic voyage toward Paradise.

It soon became apparent that Paradise was still a long way away. Certainly farther than the offshore route toward Norfolk. Dean sat next to me in the cockpit, staring forward intently, as if forcing himself not to look aft, toward the life he was leaving behind. I tried to lift him out of his uneasiness. " Should be a broad reach to Norfolk and this time of year wind direction usually holds. Report says 15-20, but off the wind we should be fine in that." Dean nodded and forced a tight smile. I think I hid the fact that I, too, was nervous. It wasn't the crew. It wasn't even the time of year, really. It was that boat. The boat was not meant for this. Going offshore in a DreamAway 45 was like entering an MG Midget in a demolition derby. You were real short on resilience.

Suddenly, I heard a strange whirr. It was like no sound I'd ever heard at sea before. It was mechanical, but somehow foreign. It sounded like a large pump going berserk. It overwhelmed both the sound of the engine and the generator, which Dean had left running. I shot toward the companionway and stopped abruptly. Down in the main salon I saw pink fur and go-go boots. And the Hoover vacuum slurping up donut crumbs from the blue shag carpeting. We may have been headed offshore through the shipping lanes, with a green crew on a marine Winnebago, but it was business as usual for Marjorie.

We raised the mainsail and rolled out the genoa, cut the engine and generator and *Robin's Egg* moved ahead with a very small bone in her teeth. A hummingbird bone, perhaps. The boat just didn't sail, but that didn't surprise me. And we *were* moving. Even a block of wood will blow downwind. Two hours later, about 10 miles out of Newport, I checked the Loran and got an accurate fix. That was good. The wind had indeed stayed aft of the beam at 15 knots, as the weather man had said. That, too, was good. Sasha, Tasha and Marjorie had stayed below. So, except for some very strange creaks, things looked just fine.

This lasted for about an hour. Then the wind, still aft, began to freshen. Now, to a real offshore sailing vessel, this might have been slightly noticeable. But aboard a DreamAway 45 it was the Hurricane of '38. She groaned like the haunted house at Disney World. She tracked like a drunken sailor. The helm responded as if the rudder cables were rubber bands. And belowdecks looked like the aftermath of a bad frat party. Freestanding lamps, drawers, TV and plants were blended into a pile that moved back and forth across the center of the shag-carpeted salon. The door of the microwave opened and closed with a life of its own. Seawater squirted through the seals of the poorly made hatches in the galley and salon. The Hoover vacuum, now seemingly possessed, moved about on its own.

All of this brought Marjorie, Sasha and Tasha, (once again tucked into Marjorie's coat) on deck. They were all very quiet and wide-eyed. They stared out at the four-foot seas as if they were tidal waves.

"Why is it like this?" Marjorie said, finally, in the general direction of Dean and me. And then, with a look of one who had just entered a black void, she shrieked, "Where is the land? Holy God, where the hell is the goddamn land?" She searched frantically around the empty horizon. I figured that, being just a temporary guest and not being paid for any sort of instructive skills, I'd better defer to Dean on that one. But he only gripped the cockpit coaming and stared forward.

"You get waves at sea, " I said finally. "Goes with the territory. And the land's there, you just can't see it." I looked closely at Marjorie, perhaps for the first time. I noticed that she was really quite attractive, except for her present green color, which was fading now to a very pale green, like what you'd get if you blended tapioca pudding with pea soup. The two dogs with only their heads sticking out under Marjorie's chin gave the whole picture an odd alien appearance. Sasha gave me a look that would stop an LNG tanker. Suddenly, with a strange high-pitched sort of cough, Sasha threw up. And she did it in Tasha's face. This triggered a chain reaction. Tasha threw up on Marjorie. And Marjorie threw up on her knees. Then they all went below, rather quickly.

This was not the first time I'd seen vomit at sea and I didn't dwell on the subject. I had turned my attention back to the helm, or lack of helm. Sailing a DreamAway 45 was like riding a bronco. You hung on and hoped. I was, however, beginning to get used to it, learning to compensate for the boat's tendency to spin out. I began to wonder just how much rudder I had under me. And how much keel for that matter. At any rate, I told myself, we were still being blown toward Norfolk. Downhill. And at two hundred dollars a day.

Dean, I now realized, needed some perking up. I didn't think he was seasick, only anxious. That was good. In an anxious state he could help me; seasick he could not. And, if the seas increased, which they seemed to be doing, I felt sure this particular DreamAway would sink to new depths. I tried to think of something to say to get his spirits up. He looked inconsolable, but it was worth a shot.

"What plans do you have after we reach Norfolk? I ventured.

Dean turned his head toward me, collapsing the right side of the hood of his yellow slicker against his right eye and nose. He was pale, wet, cold and sick. Not a happy camper. Finally he spoke.

" A hot bath and a Holiday Inn would be a start," he said. Then a large ill-intentioned wave smacked *Robin's Egg* broadside, sending thick, cold, Atlantic spray over us both. The boat shivered through to her very soul. Below deck it must have sounded like the inside of a Chinese gong.

And then there was another sound. It was a hard rapping noise right under our feet. I looked toward Dean.

"It's my wife," he said. "Whenever she wants me she takes one of the lamps from the bed table under us and bangs on the ceiling. I'd better go see what she wants."

Five minutes passed and he returned on deck. On his face was a look that eclipsed all expressions of hopelessness I'd ever seen. It was pure resignation.

"She wants to run around" was all he said,

"She wants to *what?*"

"She wants to turn around."

"But that's upwind. Ninety miles upwind. In this particular boat.

Then it came, "Well, *we* want to turn around " he said.

And that is what we did. For it was his boat.

For 14 hours, we pounded and lurched into sharp head seas with the big diesel engine. Water cascaded over the bow, liquid avalanches sliding toward that big DreamAway windshield. I can't imagine what it must have been like below deck. For a while Dean steered, his face blank. Hour after tedious hour, the slapping and pounding went on. But it was only a matter of time and diesel fuel until we picked up the sight of land. After we passed Block Island, we powered on a little faster in smaller seas.

As I sat there looking at Dean, I did a lot of thinking about the reality of romance. And finally I just blurted out a few thoughts. "Really, Dean," I said, "there is no more romance in French Polynesia, than there is in Gary, Indiana. It's all a state of mind. Hell, there's probably more romance in reading a Conrad novel than visiting a thousand Tahitis. Or in just sailing the bay. Have you ever cruised to the Elizabeth Islands, or out to Block Island, watching those cliffs approach at the end of the day? Why don't you think about starting smaller?"

Dean wiped some spray from his face and looked at me with the first piece of a smile I'd seen in 24 hours. "Maybe you are right," he said. "But right now, all I can think about is a secure marina, a hot shower, and a stiff drink."

I smiled back at him and nodded.

Ah, Paradise!

FINDING THE LIGHT

Eight or nine miles out, in plain sight, Boon Island lifts its solitary shaft aloft like an 'eternal exclamation mark' to the temerity of its builders. There is no comfortable dwelling on that lonely rock, over which storms sweep unchecked. The tower is itself both house and home to the watchmen of the sea, and in great gales a prison from which there is no escape until the return of fine weather.
Samuel Adams Drake, *The Pine Tree Coast*, 1891

It was dark and Bill and Sarah had been at sea for about thirteen hours on an August night in 1987. They had been able to carry sail all day in their newly-acquired 30 foot ketch, sailing into a light southerly breeze from Maine toward home in Massachusetts. Now, darkness had descended and with it the wind dropped, so they were under power moving at six knots with just the mainsail up. Bill had his eyes fixed on the light of infamous Boon Island, where the British ship *Nottingham Galley* met her fate on December 11, 1710, her crew struggling to stay alive on the ice covered and lonely rock for over three weeks, finally resorting to cannibalism to survive.

Sarah was standing in the cockpit facing forward in the darkness, feeling the light summer breeze on her face when they hit Boon Island Ledge. They hit with such force that one of Sarah's knees smashed into the bridge deck, the resulting lump growing to the size of a grapefruit.

Bill had figured his course that morning from the mouth of the Sheepscott River in Maine; he determined that if he sailed a generous distance to the seaward side of Boon Island, he'd miss both Boon and its outer Boon Island Ledge and also get a more direct course to the Isles of Shoals, where they planned to stop and rest. But, though the night was clear, Bill couldn't seem to find the Ledge's red flashing light. As he became more and more anxious, he began altering course increasingly toward Boon Island itself, figuring from his large scale chart that he would be in safer water when closer to Boon Island than to Boon Island Ledge. He never did see the Ledge's light, even after they hit. Sarah didn't see it either, for she is blind.

Here's the scene from Sarah's perspective. She's facing the evening breeze, smelling the sea air, feeling the ketch's undulating motion in the long swell and the vibration from the engine. Though she can't help Bill find the light, she's there in company and spirit. Sarah loves sailing and the work of sailing; she's always been an adventurous person. The close quarters of a boat are much easier for her to assimilate than is the broader world. She knows every spot on board: all the distances and steps and places for lines and gear. She's not afraid of the foredeck. And the galley is easier than cooking at home; everything is in a small space with everything in its place. Finally, at day's end, she welcomes making harbor, where her keen senses pick up the subtle change in motion, the first smell of shore, and the joyous sound of the song sparrow.

When they hit the ledge, Sarah's senses went on high alert. "My first and constant thought after we hit was DON'T GET SEPARATED FROM BILL. I knew if I let go of Bill I would be truly alone and helpless. I knew if we got separated, I would drown. Actually, I was sure we were both going to drown anyway. I could hear water pouring into the main cabin."

Bill had other things on his mind. He couldn't radio for help, as they'd lost their VHF antennae in a blow off Seguin Island several days earlier. He told Sarah to sit tight and he shot below. On the way, he reached into the cockpit cooler to feel for bottled water, but all he found was beer. Below deck, he grabbed chart, compass, flare gun and am/fm radio. Then he headed to the forepeak and grabbed his banjo. "When he handed me that banjo," Sarah said, "I thought: Gee, Bill must think we're not going to die!"

The two of them got into their 7'5" dinghy and rowed a safe distance from the ketch as she sank down to her rails. But Bill wanted to go back, climb on the foredeck, and throw out an anchor, in hopes of a later salvage. He reasoned that if the ketch could be 'anchored on the bottom' after she sank, she'd stay put and not be swept away by the undersea ocean currents; then he could come back later and perhaps raise her. But, as he tried to climb aboard, the ketch, now with too much water in her, began to roll dramatically, threatening to overwhelm and swamp their small dinghy, so Bill let go.

They rowed away. Bill took bearings, observed wind and waves, and determined that the light they could just see on the mainland was Cape Neddick. They had to choose between going to the nearby but abandoned Boon Island or to Cape Neddick. "The decision was easy," Bill said, "I had just read the book *Boon Island* and the horrifying story of the cannibalism there after the shipwreck. So that made the decision a quick one for me. You see, the person who gets eaten is the ship's carpenter. I'm a carpenter."

They took shifts at rowing. They developed a system for carefully changing seats after one tired of the oars. As the wind began to pipe up, they made less progress, and they feared their tiny dinghy would soon swamp. They had rowed about five miles and still had two to go. To get their minds off their fear, they played a game. "This is what saved us psychologically," Sarah said. "We are both musicians as well and know quite a few tunes. So the game was that in turn we had to come up with a song that began with each letter of the alphabet; we disallowed *Fiddlers' Green* when we got to 'F'. We made it all the way to 'W' (*We shall overcome*)."

"At 5 am Bill saw a lobster boat in the distance and shot off two flares and we frantically waved a jacket, but the boat continued on. At 9 a.m. another boat passed and then suddenly turned around. It was a cruising sailboat from Portsmouth. They had thought we were kayakers and dismissed us, but all our waving finally changed their minds."

After the rescue, friends organized a concert fundraiser and Bill and Sarah used the money to hire a vessel with side scan sonar to find their boat. But the ocean currents had done their work and the ketch, which had also been named Sarah, was gone.

* * *

It's many years later, December 2009, just before Christmas, and we're sitting in their cozy antique kitchen in Salem, Massachusetts as I conduct this interview. A gentle snow is falling. The kitchen fireplace adds even more warmth to the room. I find out there is another sailboat now, a 33 footer. "Sarah sails her on as steady a course as anybody can," Bill says. "She steers to the voice of a talking compass designed by an electrical engineer friend who is also blind." He pauses and pokes the fire. "Oh, and I should tell you we are just now building a house for ourselves in Maine. Doing it together. By hand. And you should see Sarah handle a nail gun when she puts up those shingles," he says proudly, looking over at his wife, who's making some soup for herself, tea for me, and occasionally patting her guide dog. Sarah returns his compliment with an infectious, knowing and gracious smile. Then it's quiet for a moment, save for the crackling fire. And in that moment, I think to myself: there's more light in this world than I ever imagined.

FAITH, FEAR AND FATE

The strong southeast winds had not dropped with the sun as they usually did in July, and the threatening black ledges thirty yards from *Elsa's* stern off barren Smuttynose Island were close enough to show their barnacles as each wave receded. Peter hooked the long pennant of an unknown mooring that seemed sizable enough, but, combined with what I knew about Smuttynose's history, there was nothing calming about our arrival. I thought of both faith and fate: my faith in each unknown link of that mooring chain; my faith in the tightness of each shackle pin down there connecting us to the mooring gear. Who had cast the chain? And how long ago? Who had tightened the shackle pins? Oh, well, it was just another case of fate ruling the day.

Then I thought of the faith and fate of two women who had lived and died on the island 90 feet away in the early hours of March 6, 1873. The only structure now on the Isles of Shoals' island of Smuttynose was the small clapboard caretaker's house, staffed by two volunteers. I looked at the flickering kerosene lantern light, now visible in one window. Nearby once stood the weather beaten red house that sheltered a hardy pioneering Norwegian fisherman named John Hontvet and his wife Maren. They had later been joined by Karen, Maren's sister, who had also emigrated from Norway. Last to join the growing family in the small house were Even and his beautiful new bride Anethe. Fishing was an isolated, lonely, and hard way to eke out a living off the remote small island. But it was better than the starvation that had faced them in Norway. Slowly things seemed to get better; John was saving money and

Maren was less lonely with the two women with her now, especially while John and Even were at sea. Then, on March 5, 1873, John and Even had to sail into Portsmouth for bait, which was arriving by train from Boston. The train was late, forcing them to spend the night tied to the wharf in Portsmouth, leaving the three women alone on Smuttynose for the night. John had faith that the women would be fine without the men for just one night. But Louis Wagner, a desperate out-of-work drifter also in Portsmouth that evening, learned of the situation, stole a dory and rowed the ten miles to Smuttynose, most likely with robbery and perhaps rape on his mind. Things went horribly wrong; two of the three women, Anethe and Karen, were brutally murdered by ax in the pre-dawn hours. Maren escaped and ran barefooted in her nightshirt to the other end of the island, hiding in a cave while clinging to her small dog. Louis Wagner searched for Maren, the only living witness, but figured she would die of exposure and, fearing the light of day, he rowed back to Portsmouth.

No part of this story made for a cozy sleep on *Elsa*. Rum helped a bit. The next morning the wind stayed strong out of the southeast, so Peter and I put a single reef in the main, dropped the mooring pennant, and headed east for Casco Bay. We've been sailing together for 35 years, so we are a pretty coordinated team. Still, putting the reef in at the mooring was a chore; maybe better to do it underway with a load on the sail and less slapping around, I thought. But, then again, I didn't know what the seas would be like when we rounded the corner. So I figured this to be safer. After Peter threw off the pennant, I had to motor into the 25 knot wind to get around the point of Appledore Island. Peter checked the reefing lines at the mast and then headed aft. As he stepped from the deck to the cockpit, the frantically slatting mainsail lifted and then dropped, the large aluminum boom crashing into Peter's head.

If fate were different, he'd be dead. Another quarter inch drop of the boom and its full weight would have split his head open, knocked him unconscious and perhaps over the side. Instead, my friend fell to the cockpit seat, wide eyed and staring. Blood streamed from the top of his head and down his forehead. "Don't let me go to sleep," he said. "Give me a minute and a lot of paper towel, and I think I'll be ok." I circled back toward the dock on neighboring Star Island, just in case. But he *was* ok. And, after making certain, we continued on to Casco Bay.

On the offshore leg I thought about it a lot. I thought about what could have happened amidst the swirling circumstance of life. And then I thought about Anethe and Karen and their fate. If Louis Wagner had been on a different street in Portsmouth that night and not heard about the women being alone; if John and Even had picked up the bait on a different day; if the train from Boston had been on time.

Just then Peter started to come up on deck, pulling his cap down tight over some squished paper towel on his head. "I guess I just got lucky on this one, Dave," he said, smiling.

"Luckier than Louis Wagner and those two women," I replied.

"Yeah, what finally did happen to Wagner? You never told me."

"Let's just stay he succumbed to a stiff neck, with limited ground support by the hands of the law," I said.

A doubled-up sea lifted *Elsa's* stern higher than usual, and she dipped into the next swell. It was more than a frolic. It was getting rougher. I should pay more attention to the helm now. No more mistakes. But I had one last thought as I looked at my friend in the companionway:

"And Peter, before fate finishes you off completely, put a proper bandage and some Bacitracin on that cut, will you?"

The Rewards of Uncertainty

Some of the by-products of adulthood should be caution, contingency planning, calculation and reservation. It's a tough world. But, in this modern age, are we getting so forewarned and cautious that we sacrifice the vitality of adventure or some of the primal thrill of the double dare? I remember talking to a friend with a marina-tethered sailboat last year. "Going out today?" I asked. "Nice breeze blowing."

He looked up at the sky, saw a bit of haze and a few looming clouds. "Don't think so," he replied. " My back-up GPS is on the fritz." He paused. "I'd love to go" he said. "I really would, but there could be some fog later. You never know."

That's true: you never know. But in always hesitating, we can never really go anywhere.

As Goethe wrote:

Until one is committed, there is hesitancy, the chance to draw back, always ineffectiveness. Concerning all acts of initiative and creation there is one elementary truth, the ignorance of which kills countless ideas and splendid plans: That the moment one definitely commits oneself, then Providence moves too. All sorts of things occur to help one that would never otherwise have occurred.

In the "olden days," cruising was very much a controlled adventure and much more vital to my soul. The uncertainty was great. The hope enormous. And the rewards were supreme. Navigation was always a challenge. Charts were paper, often faded or smudged, and sometimes as hard to read as a treasure map.

Deviation on the compass had to be factored in. Speed, distance and drift had to be calculated. Depth of the water under us was often unknown or uncertain. Yet when I look at 40 years of cruising – before GPS, instant weather radar, digital depth and bottom contour-reading technology and immediate cell-phone communication – the experiences I truly value are still these: Learning to swing a lead line as we worked our way in close to shore, reading the bottom's condition for best anchoring places by looking at whether mud, sand or nothing at all was in the indented bottom of the lead; learning to determine speed, current and drift by dropping a Coke bottle off the bow and watching its movement as it floated by; determining how close we were to shore by shouting through a cardboard megaphone and listening for voice echoes; and finally, sitting silently in our old wooden cutter after making harbor in the fog, having been challenged by the mystery of our location, and having utilized all the elements at hand to find the treasure that was our destination. For me, there was magic and joy in finding a buoy or making a harbor using only native instincts and whatever other resources could be summoned. Even the act of communicating to loved ones upon our safe arrival was an adventure. It usually meant sitting under kerosene lamps in the cozy cabin while waiting our turn for the ship-to-shore telephone operator to place the call. A bonus was the chance to eavesdrop on this public frequency on the often way-too-personal calls of other boaters. And sometimes, when we had no marine telephone reception, we would venture ashore to find a land line. This often meant wandering down a dirt road, knocking on a door of a private home, and entering the lives of locals who would otherwise have remained unknown to us in their shore-side world.

To me, cruising has been about escaping our often predicable daily lives. It is a controlled adventure, an experience of hope, expectation, surprise and reward. Try it sometime. Unplug everything and go. Commit to this and, as Goethe wrote:

A whole stream of events will issue from this decision, raising in one's favor all manner of unforeseen incidents and meetings and material assistance, which no man could have dreamed would have come his way. Whatever you can do or dream you can, begin it. Boldness has genius, power and magic in it.

IN SEARCH OF SIMPLICITY

I recycled my marine-supply-company catalog yesterday without reading any of it. It ran 1000 pages and contained 50,000 items. Supposedly those items were all there to allow the consumer a myriad of choices to facilitate his ability to get away, go boating, relax and be happy. I wonder, though.

Robert Bellah, one of today's most influential sociologists and recipient of the National Humanities Medal from President Clinton wrote:

That happiness is to be attained through limitless acquisition is denied by every religion and philosophy known, but it is preached by every American TV set.

How much do we really need to acquire before these things eclipse the value and beauty of our original quest, which is often the simplicity of just going out on the water?

Over a decade ago, way Downeast and lost in the densest of dungeon fog in my tiny sloop *Chang Ho*, I unwittingly sailed out of our modern world and into one man's world of true simplicity. My friend Bryan and I had come 150 miles off shore, a long way on a sloop with an 18-foot waterline. "You know," I said to Bryan one night, as he loaded the ninth set of AA batteries into "Geepers," my handheld GPS, "with all these electronic gizmos — autopilot, GPS, radar, assorted interfaces — one could preprogram the whole vacation and then send *Chang Ho* cruising without us. We could strap a camcorder above the nav station, point it at the radar screen, and interface with GPS and autopilot. Then, via satellite dish and cellular phone, we could sail Chang Ho from my living room couch while eating chips and watching the ball game!"

Ah, but the wonders of modern technology, I mused, as I watched Bryan pick up his battered copy of L. Francis Herreshoff's "The Compleat Cruiser", a book published long before the proliferation of electronic gizmos. Bryan, a man who'd rather be studying a piece of igneous intrusion from Grand Manan Island than programming a GPS, looked down at the plastic box and shook his head. "Does this thing really make cruising better? 'Better,' I mean... in the Zen sense?" He paused. He put down his beloved book, and looked me in the eye. "I liked *Chang Ho* and cruising with you in Maine when things were a little closer to the edge."

Closer to the edge. Maybe he was right. Maybe we needed more adventure and less predictability. Predictability is, after all, boring. Maybe we needed to 'kick it up a notch'.

Earlier that year, in January, while perusing the charts one cold night, I discovered what looked like the Holy Grail of remote, obscure Maine coves. And that following summer, when I asked a crusty-looking cruising guy on a wooden Atkin ketch if he'd heard of it, he just smiled. Then, as he was rowing away, he winked at me.

"Just promise to keep it to yourselves," he said finally.

Anyway, *Chang Ho*, Bryan and I finally found Heron Cove at the end of another fog-heavy day. We dropped the hook, and sat quietly in the cockpit, spellbound by the beauty and tranquility around us. Imagine an unspoiled, deepwater river that leads to a smaller, unspoiled uninhabited tributary, which in turn leads into a small wilderness-rimmed deepwater cove that at high tide leads into an even smaller cove with 6 feet at low tide in the center and room enough for one boat. Throw in a sun-warmed stream for washing, blueberry and raspberry fields, several bald eagles, and you've got Heron Cove. Don't bother looking it up because you won't find it. Only those who've been there know its real name, and once you've been there, you'll call it Heron Cove, too. That is, of course, *if* you find it.

The next morning we explored the blueberry fields, and inspected an abandoned trapper's shack. I wondered how many decades ago that trapper had lived there, and I wondered if anyone had been there since. Apart from the eagles, we were completely alone: no sound, no sign of humanity. It was easy to get used to. I was in awe of our isolation.

Then, out of a tidal hole in the trees slid an ancient, 20-foot wooden canoe. I blinked hard and rubbed some fog dew from my eyelashes just to make sure. Standing in the stern was a lanky man in his 60s. His clothes were ragged. His long, thin hair was disheveled. From his precarious standing position he took long, careful strokes with what must have been an eight foot paddle, moving the slender craft easily and gracefully by, paying me no notice. He disappeared in the fog by the entrance to the cove. I wasn't sure if I'd really seen anything. It had been a very long cruise lost in the fog, and I was getting used to imagining things that weren't there.

Several hours later, on the return tide, I watched the canoe re-enter the cove and then disappear into the tidal hole in the woods. "Bryan," I announced, "we're going in there."

"No, *you're* going in there," he said. "You forget it's close to dusk, and those deep woods mosquitoes take no prisoners. The only thing they'd find would be our Tevas."

I had to admit he was right.

The next morning I rowed in, and found a 20-acre pool circled by more dense woods. No sign of canoe. No sign of life. Then I spied something sticking out of the trees. It was the canoe. I eased the dinghy over closer. What the woods covered was a lean-to filled with firewood; ancient-looking cookware hung to its sides. Next to that was a big, stone-rimmed campfire surrounded by handmade stools and chairs. When the dinghy touched the shore, it seemed as if the crunching sound would wake the universe.

"Might as well stay for a bit."

The voice from the trees startled me. A hand reached out from the bushes. I handed it the bowline and stepped ashore.

"I saw you in the canoe last evening," I blurted. "Is this your land?"

He moved silently to one of the handmade chairs, and motioned me to do the same. He sat and gently stroked a caterpillar which was inching along his outstretched arm.

"Far as the eye can see," came the reply finally.

"How long do you stay here?" I asked, figuring it to be a week-end retreat.

"All the time."

"All summer, then?"

"All year."

I looked over at the lean-to and the Spartan supplies, thinking of the harsh Maine winters and how that would be impossible.

"All year? Really? For how long have you been doing that?"

"Thirty five years."

He winked at the caterpillar, and then looked up at me, a gentle smile on his face and a timeless look in his eyes. "Would you like to see the yurts?"

"The yurts?"

"Yes, the yurts."

We walked along a pine-needled carpeted path, over a stream, and through a flowering meadow. And there, in the midst of a clearing in the pines, stood a gigantic structure comprised of three stacked concentric circles. It looked like an alien space-ship that had found its perfect landing spot in these remote woods.

He lifted his arm toward it. "Know much about yurts?" he asked. My eyes were wide with amazement. I was speechless. "Guess not," he continued. "Well, come on in and you soon will." The outermost circle had a dirt floor. One section was filled with cords of neatly stacked firewood; the remaining area housed enough hand- and leg-powered drills, saws, and lathes to outfit a cabinet shop. "Built the whole thing with these simple

human-powered tools; no need for electricity" he said. We walked up several steps and entered the next circle, which was the living unit. It was furnished with comfortable, hand-built chairs and couches. The floor was covered with felt pads and carpets. Books were shelved in every conceivable space. A long, low woodstove, used for both heating and cooking, jutted into the center of the living area. Another set of stairs led up into the middle circle, which was a sort of glass-rimmed cupola. It was the master bedroom. Perhaps thirty feet up, it commanded a spectacular view of the wilderness around us, which I now saw contained guest yurts, storage yurts, and even a yurt outhouse. Before me lay Yurtdom.

The man spoke softly. "We need an enlightened time. A time when people truly question everything that is labeled 'progress'. We don't take enough time to look back at the wisdom of the past. It's so simple. We need to learn from the old and not be so quick to jump at the new for its very newness. The old is time-tested. The new is as fraught with the potential for disaster or chaos as it is with promise. Take yurts: yurts are ancient dwellings used by Mongolian pastoral nomads of Central Asia. They've stood the test of time. You're standing in a perfect example. We need to take advantage of — and not forsake — all that history has taught us about ourselves and the way we live. You see, if we don't look back at what we've learned in the past and apply that knowledge, we'll make tragic mistakes in the future. We can't just devour newness and new things."

I tried to look pensive and take all this into my tiny brain. "So we've got too much stuff," I said finally.

"Civilization, in the real sense," he replied, "consists not in the multiplication of wants but in their deliberate reduction. This alone promotes happiness and contentment."

I was amazed by the thoughts of this wizard in the woods. "Did you just come up with that saying," I asked.

"Some guy named Gandhi said it first," he replied and smiled. Then he looked down and gently stroked something yellow on his arm. It was the caterpillar.

And it was safe with him.

FLY AWAY, OLD BUDDY

I'm not sure any of you will believe my tale, but since only Bryan and I were present at the time of this death at sea, I need to tell my side of the story.

I am not an angry man, and certainly not a murderer. In fact, never in my life have I engaged in any sort of violent behavior. Bryan seems to believe otherwise. Even now, a year later, I sense his suspicion of me. And I sense his visceral fear and anger. I sense it whenever he happens to be in front of me: on a busy street corner, near an open window, or, as he was last week, when he stood with his back to me on the high cliff way above Halibut Point that looks east toward Isles of Shoals. I think he wonders: will I kill again? This is why I must tell this story.

It was late in the fall. November. Too late to be delivering *Opus*, his 26-foot Frances sloop, from Maine back to Marblehead. There was an edge to the air that spoke to me. "Make it quick: don't linger, stupid; you shouldn't be out here in the first place." I pretended not to hear, and got busy raising the main. After all, Kennebunkport to Marblehead isn't that far.

The recently rebuilt single-cylinder Yanmar sounded good, and we had plenty of warm clothes and food. A long languorous swell rolled under us on its way toward George Bush Sr.'s summer compound as we putt-putted out the channel. We rolled out the tanbark genoa, killed the one-lung iron beast, and, in a welcome silence, fell off on our course toward Cape Ann.

About an hour later the silence was broken by a light metallic hammering coming from the mast. It didn't sound like a rapping halyard; more like an anemic mini-jackhammer. I worked my way forward to investigate. On the forward side of the mast, about four feet off the deck, oblivious to me and very intent on his business, was a small bird. He pecked frantically at the aluminum mast, hoping, I suspect, to find an insect or two burrowed within. As you might guess, he wasn't having any luck.

"What'd you find?" Bryan asked as I returned to the cockpit.

"Well, there's a bird up there, and he's either soft in the head or he's found some real tasty termites living in your anodized aluminum mast."

The wind shifted a bit, dropped off a lot, and we started the engine. After powering for a few minutes, we noticed the bird take flight from the mast and circle broadly around us before coming to land on top of the dodger. He was clearly tired, hungry, and maybe lost or disoriented. We stared at him, and he back at us. Then he took off again, circled, and landed on the starboard cockpit winch. Again, the three of us stared at one another, cocking our heads, aliens unable to communicate.

"You hungry and tired, little guy? I asked the bird. " No," Bryan interjected, "he's just here to pick up his dry cleaning on the way to a bird convention in Miami."

Wise guy. The bird hopped to the bottom of the boat's small cockpit foot well. Then he hopped up on the toe of one of my boots, settled there for a while, and then – and I'm not making any of this up – he hopped onto Bryan's right knee.

As the day went on we became very attached to our new feathered friend, and he seemed to feel the same way about us. We named him Buddy. We tried to feed him tiny bits of crackers, but with no luck. Buddy seemed to be happy just to have found a space that didn't require wings. In fact, I think *Opus* became his dream boat. He began to hop around like an integral part of the crew, alighting on the deck, the dodger again, back to the winch, and finally, back to the cockpit sole, my boot and Bryan's knee.

After my watch I decided to take a nap and ducked below to the warmth of the vee berth. I was asleep in seconds but later awoke to Bryan's voice. " Pssst...pssst...David... don't move, but open your eyes — Buddy's sleeping under your chin." Sure enough, our new friend had burrowed between my beard and under my down jacket top and appeared to be blissfully asleep. And so it went. It seemed Buddy had now decided that being in the cabin was best of all, and he flitted about the cozy space, hopping about and alighting on the kerosene lamp, the stove, the bookshelf and the quarter berth.

Meanwhile, we went about our shipboard business. At some point between passing Boon Island and Isles of Shoals Bryan asked me to grab his bird guide from the bookshelf, so we could iden-tify our new shipmate. Below, I noticed Buddy sitting happily on the tattered Maine Coast cruising guide as I reached into the line of books and grabbed the bird book. We identified him as a red-breasted nuthatch. About that time we also started to look for the entrance buoy to the Annisquam River off Cape Ann. I tossed the thick paperback guide below and grabbled the binoculars to iden-tify the buoy. It was now just before dark and getting really cold. It started to drizzle. But I knew we'd make it in OK within the hour, grab a mooring in the cove off the little village of Annisquam, start the stove/heater, pour some good rum, and get warmed up. Fifteen minutes later I went below to grab the small-scale chart for Bryan, then tidied up the small cabin to make it a bit more welcoming for our landfall. I didn't see Buddy.

"Bummer. Must have flown off when we got closer to land," Bryan said. "I thought he'd be with us forever. What a cool little guy."

"Weird," I said. "I just saw him down below decks about 15 minutes ago. Must have flow away while we were searching for the buoy."

The Annisquam light was just visible in the drizzle and dying light of day. We would be moored soon. One of the very few advantages of boating in November is the abundance of empty moorings. Once secure on one we dove into the cabin, lit the stove and kerosene lantern, and poured our rum. Things warmed up in no time. Our thoughts turned back to Buddy.

"We were never that far from land. Why would he stay with us all day and then suddenly disappear?" Bryan asked. He seemed truly crestfallen.

"Maybe he didn't," I said "Let's look around some more." But we found nothing. Later, while the stew was simmering, Bryan asked me to reach forward into the bookshelf to grab the bird book again.

"Maybe we missed something about him," he said. " I want to read more about nuthatches. He was such a cool little guy."

Reaching into the shelf, I lifted out the thick bird book. The adjacent paperbacks toppled, and when I reached in to prop them back up, my hand felt something soft and round. I grabbed the flashlight, pointed it to the spot and flipped it on.

I didn't say anything for several moments, letting the pieces come together for me. Bryan was busy with a large knife, cutting carrots for the stew.

Finally, I spoke. " Ah Bryan?... Ah, I just found Buddy... And, ah, well, he's kind of dead."

Bryan moved forward in a flash. He turned to me, knife still in hand. The dancing glow of the kerosene lantern gave his face a contorted Jack Nicholson "The Shining" kind of look in the half darkness.

"Sorry, man," I croaked. " He must have snuggled into the space left from the bird book when you had it in the cockpit. Then, when I was tidying up, well, I put the book back. I must have sort of squished him with it. Jesus, I killed the freaking bird with a bird book. How weird is that?"

Bryan was in no mood for discussing what was weird. "No. You didn't kill him. You murdered him," he said. "You murdered Buddy."

It was the beginning of a long uneasy night. "Quit kidding man," I'd say over and over through the rest of the rum bottle. "Stop calling me a murderer. You're weirding me out."

But he never has. The next day, on the last leg to Marblehead, after covering Buddy's body with a tiny canvas shroud, we buried him at sea. We sent him to the thereafter by sliding his tiny lifeless form through *Opus's* starboard scupper. "Ashes to ashes, feather to feathers," I said in prayer, trying to lighten the moment.

Bryan watched for a long time as Buddy's tiny body disappeared in our wake. Then he turned to me.

"Murderer," he said.

WASTE NOT, WANT NOT

Thousands, maybe millions, of seagulls, geese, cormorants, ducks and fish poop into the water all around me twenty-four hours a day when I go cruising. But my waste is *human* waste, which apparently is a special excrement and needs a holding tank. I don't think this is fair, though I do realize the challenge in retrofitting seagulls, geese, cormorants, ducks and fish with holding tanks.

The idea of storing 20 gallons of human excrement under my bunk, six inches below my pillow has never appealed to me. Humans invented this concept: place a 20-gallon plastic box or rubber bladder under the boat's forward bunk, connect it with lots of hoses — one for intake from the head, one for pump-out, one for overboard discharge, and one for venting —and there you go. All nice and tidy. Then go sailing. Bounce over big waves, shake it all about, even add to it as you go, if you feel the urge. At the end of the vigorous day, climb into your bunk above it all. Turn in for the night in the forepeak. Listen to the sloshing. Smell the air. Ah, romance.

No thanks. My entire holding-tank system and its leaky, easily clogged head and I were finished. I was switching to a small, self-contained Porta Potti. I served the entire system an eviction notice in the winter of 2007, and then I waited for one of the coldest days of that winter to effect removal. There was a reason for this: I'd heard horror stories of holding tank hoses letting go, liberating the tank's contents into the dark, impossible-to-clean regions of boats, making them virtually uninhabitable — and sometimes unsellable. Since I was doing the removing, I didn't want any accidents. My logic was simple: the intense cold would freeze any remaining waste in the system and thereby avoid any chance of a Category Five spill during the extrication. Piece of cake.

On Saturday, January 7, the temperature was 17 degrees. Perfect. Though alone at the boatyard, I sheepishly looked over my shoulder as I climbed the ladder and ducked under the tarp. I feared my mission would appear a bit odd and didn't want to answer any questions. Once aboard, I launched the attack. I removed the forward bunk cushion, and then the bunk boards underneath, exposing the top of the plastic tank. Here, I was able to remove the leather restraining straps that bound the tank to the boat. But then things began to get complicated. I couldn't lift up and remove the tank without cutting the intake and discharge hoses that connected to the tank's bottom, and I couldn't reach them from the top.

So I removed the two-foot-high by six-inch wide door from the vertical face of the forward bunk. This exposed the hoses and gave me access. Shivering in the intense cold, I reached in and cut the big discharge hose. It was then that I learned something new: treated human excrement does not really freeze at seventeen degrees. Did I begin to panic? You bet. I shot aft, frantically searching for something – anything – that could catch the flowing sludge. I found a wine bottle. I found a small plastic cup. Nothing would do. Nothing except my wife's three galley saucepans. Grabbing them, I dashed forward, dropped to my knees and, turning one of the saucepans sideways to get it through the six-inch wide door, stuck it under the offending hose, breathing a sigh of relief.

Since I thought I was sure I'd pumped out the tank in the fall, I knew the flow would soon stop. It had to. It didn't. OK, fine. Gingerly, I moved the now full saucepan to the remaining small space beside the tank and tipped and slid in another one. And still the flow came, like ooze from a Grade B horror film. With only one pan left, I began to get really nervous. I'd soon have to remove the full pans, empty them (where, I wasn't sure) and start all over again.

The second pan filled; there was just enough room to slide it over by the first and insert the third. And still it came. It was then, as with a drowning man going under for the third time, that I realized the end was coming. I felt this way because what leaked into my mind at this point was this: the only way I could remove the three full saucepans was to turn them sideways to get them back out through the opening. Understanding clearly what the result would be, I refused to suffer that final, gross indignity. So I simply got up off my knees, slowly returned to the main cabin, sat down on the port settee, and poured a shot of rum down my throat.

Epilogue: Should any of you become a dinner guest aboard my boat this summer, don't worry about any bad smells, or E. coli bacteria. The flow stopped just as the last pan filled. And my dear wife gave me new saucepans for my birthday. But if you go swimming, for God's sake watch out for the cormorant poop.

KISSING THE BRIDE

She lay languidly between the arms of Harbor and Hall Islands in the midst of ledge-strewn Muscongus Bay and, despite the disheveled condition of her captain and two mates — who had not seen the likes of soap, razors or toothbrushes in days — she held her head high. *Elsa*, my beautiful 30-year-old silk purse of a sloop, was demurely holding up three old sows' ears.

But even in the freshening southwest breeze, the air was getting ripe around us. "Hey, you guys, ah, maybe we should find a harbor with a shower tonight," I timidly suggested to my crusty crew. Bryan looked at me askance, as if I'd requested newly-laundered embroidered doilies for under our rum cups at tonight's meal.

"You know, Dave," said my old pal Peter with a lingering tinge of southern drawl. "It's not what you look like or even smell like; it's only how you act that matters." I cocked my head. He continued: "Ladies have never been bothered by me in this condition, 'cause it's all about attitude; it's all about approach. Always remember that."

"Well, I'm no lady," I said. "But not even a Big Foot beast would approach *you* right now... and I'm speaking of an ugly desperate female one."

Just then the cell phone rang. It was my son Nick, who had the weekend off and wanted to drive up and join us for a couple of days. We were flattered that a good looking, well-dressed twenty-something would want to spend time with the likes of this crew. But then he hadn't smelled us yet.

So we settled on meeting him at one of my favorite little harbors on the tip of Southport Island. There was an inn that had two moorings for rent, which was all the space there was for guest boats in this tiny harbor. We called and reserved a spot. But the lady on the phone at the inn was tentative. "I hope it's OK," she said, "but we won't be able to serve you in the dining room tonight. You see, we're hosting a big fancy wedding,"

That's ok, we said. We don't do dining rooms. The statement brought me back to the old cruising days in tiny *Chang Ho*, my Cape Dory 25. She took us offshore many times and east as far as Cutler. It got ripe aboard *Chang Ho*, too, but, for some reason, in those days we dared to venture ashore and put ourselves in close quarters with the general public in quaint harbors Downeast. We even tried entering dining rooms in the chic small inns we'd find here and there, but we never quite gained entry due to our condition. On two occasions, what they gave us (and I'm not kidding) was a small table *in* the kitchen, where we were 'seated' away from the real guests. But both times this occurred after we had regaled the patrons with tales of our adventures, while sitting on the inn's porch or at the small bar just outside the dining room. It was clear these folks were getting pretty bored with all this quiet Maine inn charm, and we, in our weather-beaten state, with our ratty foul-weather gear and salt-stained cut off jeans were ironically a breath of fresh air. In fact, at two inns a few guests even came into the kitchen to talk with us about our adventures in 'that tiny little sailboat we saw you get off'. The cooks and kitchen help jumped into the conversation too, and we all had a grand time amidst the dirty dishes and pots and pans.

But back to this story. So we headed off in *Elsa* to rendezvous with Nick in a place that seemed to be a good harbor though probably showerless. After an uneventful trip, we negotiated the extremely narrow entrance, where local knowledge tells you to squeeze through between a spindle capped by an osprey nest on your starboard and a bold rocky shore just on your port. A huge white tent came into view, set on a large manicured lawn by the harbor. Hors d'oeuvres were being served on silver trays to ladies in hats and long summer dresses and to men in white-coated wedding finery. At the foot of all this elegance was a small pier, gangway and dock. Our mooring was just off of it. I looked at my crew, the way a veteran drill sergeant looks at his fresh recruits just off the bus from their home towns. Then I looked back at the pristine picture of that separate world that lay a hundred feet away, but might as well have been a hundred miles off. "This is hopeless," I said, as we drifted up to the mooring.

A smile grew on Peter's sunburned, newly whiskered face, as he turned to address his fellow bilge scum of a crew.

"A hundred bucks to the first one of us to kiss the bride," he said.

Fortified by a bit of rum, but none the cleaner, we rowed ashore to meet Nick, who was soon to arrive by car. The wedding reception was in full swing. Baskets of flowers hung from the posts of the elegant seawall which graciously met the sloping lawn. Soft flute music emanated from the tent. Small groups of wedding guests chatted here and there on the grass, sipping from champagne flutes. It was a splendid scene.

I lost track of my crew as I slumped a bit, slinking up the hill, trying to look like a man on a mission; maybe a busy, anonymous maintenance worker.

Nick arrived on time, and now my whole crew was together on shore, halfway up the hill by the inn's pool. The aroma from the catered meal being prepared behind the tent almost eclipsed our own distinct odor, and, like four stray cats in the wrong part of town, we headed back to Elsa for our own form of shipboard cuisine.

What we hadn't counted on was the pre-planned wedding party photography on the tiny dock where we had tied our dinghy. Fortunately, they were about finished when we came down the hill. My first thought was to meld into the bushes to my right until the wedding party climbed the gangway and made its way back to the tent. I slowed my pace. Peter, however, moved forward faster, descending the hill and on a collision course with the wedding party, which was now at the top of the gangway. I slowed a bit more. Peter kept moving, into the throng of tuxedos and gowns. It was an incongruous confluence. I watched as the groom, and then the bride, looked up with increasing anxiety as Peter approached. In their faces I could sense an emerging awareness that something was wrong with this picture, as if this wedding of theirs had been a magical movie which suddenly, in its middle, contained a misplaced splice from the cutting room floor.

Then Peter's right hand came out of his ragged pocket as he moved into the midst of the wedding party and stood face-to-face with the groom, who was clearly confused by his approach. Peter, on the other hand, was grinning. Joyous. He put his left hand on the groom's shoulder and reached out and heartily shook the groom's hand with his outstretched right. "Congratulations," he said. And that's when Peter made his move. Graciously turning to the perplexed new wife in white lace, he did what is proper and should rightly follow in such a case. He stepped forward and kissed the bride.

The rest of the wedding party passed, and we headed down the gangway.

"You owe me a hundred bucks," Peter said, as we reached the small dock. Then he looked back at the festivities and smiled confidently, casually brushing aside a buzzing fly who clearly found his fragrance more alluring than that of the bride.

"And remember, Dave: It's not what you look like. Or even smell like.

It's all about the approach."

WHAT IF WHALES WEREN'T BIG?

The four of us were sitting around a mesquite-wood campfire at the base of a canyon amid the hills high above Tucson, near the old Tucson to Tombstone stagecoach road. We had spent all day in the saddle, my horse and I following Joe Valdez and his pack mule. Joe was a small grizzled man who seemed, to this East Coast sailor-man — who was in those days running a whale-watch boat — to be the epitome of the western wrangler. It was the wrong season for an overnight in the hills, but I'd talked Joe into it, saying I was an ocean guy and just had to try this.

All day during the ride, I kept trying to get Joe talking, asking what I hoped wouldn't be stupid questions. But all I ever got back were a few grunts, yups, and mebbees. That night, while intently remaining silent despite my questions, Joe cooked some tasty steaks on the mesquite fire. Coyotes howled in the darkened hills above us. A small stream bubbled past. The horses were bedded down inside an abandoned old corral. Still no talk from Joe. But quite a day, regardless.

I gave up on expecting discussion, and said I'd be turning in, which meant just slipping deeper into my sleeping bag by the fire. Joe simply nodded, continuing to poke a stick at the embers. And then, just as I was drifting off, he asked in the clearest most earnest voice "You ever seen a whale?"

Whales fascinate people. I think it's mostly because they're big. If whales were the size of mackerels, no one would care. If they hung out on the surface more, we'd probably barely notice. Whales and I have had some interesting times. The first time I saw one I was the skipper of whale-watch boat of out Salem, Massachusetts. In the pioneering days of whale watching, I was the captain, the "whale expert" and the expedition leader, all rolled into one. And I'd never seen a whale. But off I headed, bound for Stellwagen Bank, jam-packed with 135 curious souls, mostly tourists from some of those places far from whales.

"Just find the edge of the bank with the depthsounder, southeast corner, and you'll be fine," my boss said. "And here, take this," he continued, as he discreetly handed me a whale guide through the pilot house window. "You can talk about finbacks, minkes, and humpbacks, and say what a thrill it will be when they swim right up to the boat."

And that's what I talked about on the way to Stellwagen. But what I thought about was my job and what would happen to it and the $18 per head times 135 when all I found was empty ocean. In retrospect, I'm sure the tourists wondered how, in the midst of this empty ocean and empty horizon, I would know when to suddenly stop and then show them whales. I wondered this too. But finally, bless their giant hearts, there they were.

The first was a humpback and her calf. The mother even "spyhopped," coming right up under our bow and looking up with a very curious basketball-sized eye at the tourists and their cameras. One woman got really excited and blurted out to her heavyset lady friend, "My God, I think I'm having a whalegasm."

So that was the first time. There were dozens more over the next two years. Both the whales and the people came in all shapes and varieties. I even took 100 Salem witches out on their private Witch Whale Watch, though the whales were not as spellbound as the witches. I also took numerous school groups, including a high school with some tough characters. About a mile from the dock, headed out to Stellwagen on a particularly rough day, the crew chief came up to the pilothouse. "Cap, I'm getting nervous," he said. Looking over his shoulder. "These guys are eyeing the booze, the candy, even the fire extinguishers. There's a hundred of them and only two of us."

"Don't worry," I said, advancing the throttles of the big 6-110 GM diesels, then feeling the 65-foot hull begin to pitch and roll. "You'll be fine in about five minutes. Nothing like a boatload of seasickness to calm an uprising."

These days, when I sail back and forth to Maine, I'm often alone, and sometimes, I really look forward to a whale or two for company. It happens rarely, but there's always that hope that my old belly shaped 31-foot sailboat hull will prove attractive to a friendly humpback. And then, maybe if it's just the two of us out there, with no one else watching, something extra special will happen.

Why Are We Here?

For the last three days and nights there have been just two of us in here. Two boats. Two people. He's about a hundred yards away, aboard a tired 21-foot low-end cabin sailboat. One spreader droops down forlornly like the broken wing of a bird. He sits there in the tiny cockpit, smiling at nothing in particular, hands folded behind his head, listening to the osprey chicks' peeps from the nest in the trees of the small island near him, as the mother soars away looking for food. Mostly, he just watches life go by in this wondrous small bay. I too am alone, aboard *Elsa*, doing about the same thing. Neither of us, I'm sure, feel the need to communicate. Last night he started playing the fiddle. Poorly. I thought it was lovely. Perhaps he did too. For all is harmony in a place like this.

I am here awaiting new crew. I could wait forever with no anxiety or boredom. Here, as with my neighbor, I have the luxury of time to think and remember. I begin thinking about whales and their relationship to humans. When I was sailing here from Marblehead last week, a *Points East* reader who had read my last column on whales, sent me an email saying, "If you see a whale, David, could you ask him/her two questions: *Why are we here?* and *Are we going to be OK?*" It touched me as a wholly sincere question from this woman from Utah who said she'd never seen a whale but knew that they would have the wisdom of time on their side and might know the answer to this age-old question.

I think it deserves an answer, but I have yet to have that up close and personal whale talk.

At 6 a.m. and about 3 p.m. each day my neighbor on the decrepit sailboat gets in his tiny dinghy with his fishing pole, pulls out the oars, and goes fishing for dinner. It seems exactly the right thing to do. I feel a twinge of embarrassment at my own life next door. I keep marinated steak tips in my larder. He fishes for his dinner. I listen to music on my CD player. He makes his on his violin. I view the weather radar and check my emails on my fancy phone. My neighbor looks at the sky for weather, and perhaps wonders or uses his imagination to speculate how people he cares about are doing. I'm disappointed in myself that I feel oddly vulnerable that my fancy phone might die an early death and leave me with only the present. "I thought you were here to get away from all this stuff," I say out loud.

I thought about all this until late last night. My neighbor seems so content in his world. I admire that. He doesn't appear to be fleeing anything. Rather, just living. He seems to be right where he should be. Other than me, there's no one to judge him here. I sense no constraints on him. No blind ambition. Only the ambition to be where he wants to be, with whatever he has, and keep on living.

I dissect his situation. I speculate on his life. What's his job? Then I think: Why does that matter? What will you conclude and judge with that data? I try to get some perspective, but I can't. I have only my sense of what I see from afar.

What I do see is the elemental and the simple: a man connected to his world, carrying his home under him, and his shelter above him. He's in a free bay. He can probably anchor here forever if he wants. There's fish aplenty beneath him, quahogs in the mud on the shores, berries of all types on the little islands, rain squalls bringing water. In short, he is surviving. The variables in his immediate life he can count on one hand.

Five days earlier I was in another harbor, moored behind a very large and expensive sailing yacht, no doubt with the latest of everything in equipment. I watched all day as the frantic and perturbed crew tried to get their generator working. Even from a hundred feet away, I could feel the tension. You'd think it was a life or death situation. The beauty and essence of their surroundings was lost to these five people. Their reliance on this generator strangled them. No longer were they breathing in the beauty of nature. Later, the frantic five did get their generator running; the resulting exhaust drifted down into *Elsa's* cabin, and I had to get up in the rain and move up wind.

Tomorrow, I'm going to sea again. I will be away from both the simple and the complex sides of humans. I will have nothing to judge except the ocean under me. My goal will be to survive and simply move from point A to point B to complete the day's journey into the next. Kind of like the whale.

Which brings me back to that lady's questions:

Why are we here? And what will happen to us?

I promise you this, dear writer from Utah, if I see a big humpback surface next to me, I will, with reverence, raise up my palms to the sky, and ask those two questions.

Perhaps I will see the answers reflected in its huge, time-wizened eye.

WATCHING FOR ZEPHYRS

It was the end of a glorious late summer day. We had been under power, on our way back to Salem after a nice supper at the head of Marblehead Harbor, when the old Yanmar diesel started to surge. "What's going on?" my dear wife Mary Kay asked. "Is the engine breaking? You never let anything break on *Elsa*." We were still in Marblehead Harbor, and I was able to drift over to an empty mooring. The sun was setting and the fine day's west wind had gone to bed. We were four miles away from our Salem Harbor mooring. My wife had to get home soon. "Maybe we could get a tow?" she ventured hopefully. I rolled my eyes. "*Elsa* and I don't do tows," I said. Then I hailed a passing yacht club launch to take her ashore.

"You can't stay on this mooring," the launch driver said as he pulled alongside and my wife got aboard.

"Had to grab it temporarily; motor broke," I said. "Don't worry; I'm leaving right now for Salem Harbor."

"I thought you said your motor broke?" the launch driver said. By now, all the people in the launch were staring at me. I looked up and made my eyes lift slowly up to the top of my mast. Then all the people in the launch lifted their eyes slowly up to the top of my mast. I looked back at the launch driver.

"You see," I said finally, "this is actually a *sail* boat." The launch driver shook his head and gave me a "whatever" look and then gazed around at the absolutely windless harbor waters. Then he zoomed off. My wife waved goodbye from the stern of the launch as if I were headed around Cape Horn in a bathtub. I'm not sure if anyone heard me, but in a tone full of false bravado I croaked, "You see, I have a fair tide".

Heavy and somewhat sleepy, like a Saint Bernard on a hot, windless day, *Elsa* is subdued and even ill at ease in the lighter moments. But in the tough situations, on high-wind days, she's the six ton Saint Bernard you want around. Because of these attributes, I never tried to bring her to life in light air sailing situations. Instead, I would fire up her old Yanmar 2QM diesel and we would go about our business.

Things were different now, because they had to be. I had played my final hand. I had played it to my wife. I had played it to that launch driver. And I had played it to 20 or so yacht club members in his launch. I was going to drift out of Marblehead Harbor, around Peaches' Point, and up Salem Harbor if it took 'til February. I was not going to fold. I hopped forward to the mast and grabbed the main halyard. "Come on *Elsa*, we're outta here," I said.

Little did I know right then, but I was in for an epiphany. Suddenly, my senses jumped to their highest alert. Nothing mattered but the wind and the tide. My mind was absolutely cleansed of the exigencies of life ashore. Suddenly, life was all about watching for zephyrs. Looking for hints of tiny ruffles of wind, I scanned the undulating swells from the east as they rolled into Salem Sound. I searched for what Thornton Burgess' Old Mother West Wind called the "willful little Breeze who was not quite ready to go home"; the breeze that "wanted to play just a little longer."

Now, I looked up at the tell tales on the sails much more often than I looked ahead. "Men in a ship are always looking up, and men ashore are generally looking down" wrote poet John Masefield. And so, I watched for zephyrs. I became pure with nature. I was now in a world with no room for acrimony. No reason for distrust. A world that asked only one thing: that I simply pay attention. So, as nature's devoted new servant, I lived for her gifts. First, I lived only to make enough headway to reach the outer harbor of Marblehead, allowing *Elsa* to ride the incoming tide toward Salem. Then, I lived only to hook onto a little zephyr born of some lingering land warmth from Peach's Point, saving me from the nasty ledges off my bow. And, at the success of each 'life', I felt pure joy. I patted *Elsa's* teak cockpit coaming. I cheered. I shot a fist in the air. If anybody was watching, I suppose it all would have looked pretty silly, this exuberance from a lone man on a little sailboat ghosting on a flat sea at nightfall. I was just one of earth's six billion humans doing his thing. What importance could that possibly have? A lone man in harmony with nature. A lone man using every sense he can summon to make simple progress in his own little world. A lone man focused on a simple yet universal goal: to believe he can make way on his own; to feel pride at each small success along that way; to move forward, always paying attention to what the natural world is saying and offering. And, finally, to allow him to get to that place, that place in his heart or in his mind, that he calls home.

Hours later, *Elsa* drifted alongside her mooring with the last of the incoming tide, and just as the 'willful little Breeze', now tired itself, had climbed back into Mother West Wind's bag. I reached over and grabbed the mooring pick-up buoy, and walked forward with it slowly. There was no hurry. I was home.

IV

SOMEWHERE IN BETWEEN

IN THE GULF STREAM

This story is the only one in this collection not written in the first person. As you'll see when you get to the end, that's because it can't be. In 1975 I was hired by a charter company to sail a 42-foot sloop from Rhode Island to St. Thomas. I had no crew, other than my river pilot non-sailing friend Hank (who had never even <u>seen</u> the ocean) so I grabbed two boat vagrants from a bar in Edgartown. They were true reprobates, with little concern for my life, Hank's life, or their own, for that matter. I was only 25. And captain. It was my first long distance offshore voyage. Before and during the voyage, I wondered what would happen to me, and what would go through my mind, if I fell overboard in the Gulf Stream. Would these two even bother to look for me?

His first sensation was that the water was warm. For a flash his mind displayed the theme that had run through the whole trip: *At least it's not cold.* None of them had wanted to think of what the gale would have been like if it had been cold. Everything had been bad enough. The bow of their sailboat that had looked so high and mighty and protective next to the foot-high dock at the marina. What a joke. The custom galley and color coordinated dishes in their "seagoing" dish-rack. Dishes everywhere, the first day out. "Unbreakable" ones in pieces everywhere, sticking up, jabbing their bare feet, sending red and yellow plastic splinters up into their wrinkled white soles. Saltwater sores afflicting them all, starting as little red marks under the tough vinyl of their foul weather gear. Erupting later into pus-filled puffs, screaming in reaction to the rubbing, rubbing, rubbing of the protective yellow slickers that they wore constantly, even slept in because they were too tired to take them off. Eyelids red, inflamed, protruding, with soaked and matted lashes seeming only half their size. Stinging from the constant spray and solid salt water that poured over that big 'protective' bow. Ocean water that ran down the decks, and over the cabin house and invaded them, the drivers, pilots, and sailors that, strapped in and hanging on for their lives, absurdly thought they were fighting the storm.

His second thought was about the mistake he'd made. No details, only the flash that he'd gone and done the worst thing possible. That it had happened to him.

Then he saw the masthead light, like a low shooting star, cutting an arc through the black air in front of him. Five seconds had gone by since he'd fallen over, and already the boat was 40 yards away, its masthead light giving away its wildly careening motion, as the boat, shrouded in darkness, slid down a wave away from him. Frenzied, he swam, violently slamming his arms, over and over, into the sea. He was like a spring-wound toy, releasing a spasm of limited energy, trying futilely to dig through the thick carpet of sea that separated him from his only source of survival. He didn't scream, he didn't think, he only swam, his whole being utterly committed to the task of reaching the boat. His eyes stayed pinned through the spray on the white masthead light. He'd forgotten about his whistle; it hung limply in the water from his neck as he swam.

Then he lost sight of the light. Still, he kept swimming toward where it used to be, the springs of his arms and legs growing slacker and slacker, his will to live growing stronger and stronger. Then came the breakdown: his muscles began to disobey the frantic commands of his mind. Finally, he could swim no more. His head slouched back in exhaustion and rested on the buoyant collar of his lifejacket. He was unwound, there was no more strength, and he floated and bobbed in rhythm with the sea.

He could only wait and hope that the boat would find him. Had Hank seen him go over? He'd looked so white, so drained, crouched there behind the wheel. Over the past couple of days during the storm Hank had gotten so pale and skinny that he eventually became, to his strained and stinging eyes, only a yellow hooded slicker with a pale ghost of what used to be Hank inside. They were watch mates, and when not steering they had only to sit there, watch the helmsman, be ready to re-tie something, slack a sail, or take a turn at the wheel. He remembered now. A line had been banging harshly against the aluminum mast and he had climbed carefully forward, into the dark abyss of the foredeck, to tie off the snapping halyard. He'd snapped his safety harness to the jackline, which had reassured him every time he felt waves climb down from the bow toward him. The waves pummeled him, trying to wrench him loose and take him on their journey over the decks and cabin of the boat. When he'd feel a relative calm, he'd move forward again, sliding his harness snap along the jackline and ultimately clipping it to a shroud by the mast. He could sense the relative lulls, just as he could sense the freak seas, those odd breeds that would attack the boat every two or three hours. They were literally a sea on top of a sea. The top wave would not balance or stay formed, and would slide 30 or 40 feet down to the trough in a mass of churning consuming sea. The waves came with the crashing sound that breakers make when they smash themselves onto the shore in a storm.

He was snapped to the shrouds, tying off the loose halyard, when he heard it. The roar of the collapsing sea seemed to come from a great height, and he remembered debating for a moment whether to cling to the mast or try to make it quickly back to the safe well of the cockpit. Thinking back, he was surprised he had any time at all to debate what to do. It was as if the giant sea had hung over him, its frothy claws hooked over the entire boat, waiting for him to let go of the mast and make a dash for the cockpit. He never did. Instead, he clung like a bloodsucker to the thick aluminum pole. The wave hit with the solid force that tears away stone sea walls. It ripped him away from the mast and shot him into the water by the leeward side, the splice on his lifeline pulling apart like wet cardboard.

At least it's warm, he told himself again. He wondered for a few moments why he wasn't panicking anymore. And then he made himself think about the warmth again, and then of Hank's big plastic whistle. That was what he'd looked at when he didn't want to look at the seas or at Hank's ghostly face.

In Rhode Island he'd decided that they all should have whistles to wear around their necks, so that they could make sounds loud enough to pierce the wind and alert others on board in an emergency. He already had a whistle, a silver one given to a him by his wife who'd gotten it from a rape center. He remembered sending Brad and Hollis to the store to get three more. They'd taken the ship's money, bought two beautiful, expensive brass whistles for themselves and a cheap black plastic one for Hank. It hurt him that they had slighted his friend Hank that way, a person they barely knew and had no reason to dislike. He realized that taking these two strangers for the other crew had been risky. But no one else would go in late November, and whatever pirates they might be, they were good sailors. Good sailors and they'd find him. Don't panic, he told himself, they're damn good sailors. But his mind kept moving, churning with apprehension. Then he remembered the other things about them: their spending much of the provisioning money on booze, and trying to sneak it on board. He'd told them what to get and they hadn't followed orders.

He reached down to tighten his lifejacket strap, and he felt the remains of his frayed safety harness line entangled in the lifejacket adjusting buckle. He pulled on it and it seemed to knot up and only get worse He pulled again. And again. He pulled harder and it knotted harder. He pulled and pulled and pulled.

A huge lump came to his throat and like a sudden vomit, the fabric of his organized mind ripped and then exploded. He cried out. It began as a guttural choking groan that led finally to a high pitched reverberating scream. He screamed and screamed and pulled and pulled at the knot. His head went underwater and he screamed into the thick black sea. His head popped up and he screamed into the surrounding, empty night air. There were no more images in his mind now, only the blind screaming. He had no realization of anything around him. Again he had panicked.

Eventually he ran out of energy, and his head sagged back against the collar of lifejacket. For an hour he bobbed, barely conscious, conscious only enough to close his mouth when a big wave overwhelmed the tiny speck that was his head. A tiny speck in that huge ocean. A tiny speck that housed 25 years of varied experience, of accumulated life, of wealthy incident.

Dawn dispelled the nightmare of his death. He thought of what his job ahead was, and realized that there was nothing for him to do. It was a strange phenomenon. He had only to float and conserve strength. The lifejacket would float him until he rotted out of it, and there was nothing he could waste strength on. There were no alternatives but to float, bobbing away like a detached fishnet buoy. He remembered the wise man's proverb that he read somewhere: *Where there are no alternatives, there are no problems.*" What a crock of shit!

The gale was still very much with him though he barely heard the howl of the wind from his position at the bottom of the trough between the big seas. He still had on his foul weather gear, and now he tried to decide if there was any point in keeping it on. He was so used to the notion that it would protect him, that he was reluctant to remove any of the gear.

He thought for the first time of sharks, and thought of the flimsy rubber and cloth suit as protection. He thought it might hide his odor from a shark, and he thought that somehow if the water turned cold, the gear would protect him. These were his reasons. Neither was valid, but to him, they made good sense. Oddly, the only remotely sensible reason escaped him; the bright yellow of his jacket would make him more easily seen.

There were cold facts against this, however. The seas were so large that he could rarely see the horizon, and then only for a moment. His boat, or any boat, would almost have to sail over him before seeing him. He was 300 miles out in the Atlantic Ocean, his head a dot visible at a maximum of 30 or 40 yards. He was floating in the Gulf Stream, an area of frequent storms and confused, crossing seas. A ship would chop him to pieces, a plane could never get low enough to see him, and the nearest boat other than his was probably miles away. His own boat could be only one mile away and still spend a month looking and never see him.

He could only last about three days at best, and could not be seen at all except during the day. His boat couldn't maneuver in these seas, anyway. It had been all they could do just to steer away from the threatening waves. There was absolutely no reason to go on living, he had no odds, he had no chance. And if he had known this he probably would have given up and drowned. But he didn't think these realities; he was busy formulating a plan. There could be no elaborate plan, and his was a simple one. He would conserve strength at the bottom of the trough, waiting for a wave to lift him. When one would lift him to the horizon, he would put his whistle in his mouth and blow it and wave his arms madly. He thought his whistle the key to his survival and he checked the marlin cord that held it around his neck. It was strong. Good.

It was 7 a.m. He'd been in the water for eight hours. Every eight or ten minutes he'd be lifted high enough to see a short horizon, a field of a dozen or so large waves, and he would wave his arms and blow forcefully on his whistle. For hour after hour, he thought of nothing else but the boat he hoped to see on the horizon the next time he was lifted up on a wave. Of course someone would come along, he thought. Mostly likely his own boat, but maybe another yacht, a ship or a fishing trawler.

In the troughs he took stock of himself and rested between whistle blowings. The deep troughs were like a womb to him, and they became his place of thinking and reflecting. At 10 o'clock when he took stock of himself, he was encouraged. He wasn't too thirsty and he wasn't hungry, though his throat was parched. He wasn't shivering; the Gulf Stream seemed like bath water.

What if it had been Lake Superior, at 35-degree water temperature? And what if he hadn't eaten dinner right before he'd fallen over? Well prepared for this. Lifejacket. What if no lifejacket? Would have had to swim the whole time and waste valuable energy. It would have used up the food in his stomach. Well, it was still a mess, and it would take awhile to be found. Too damn bad that lifeline parted.

"World's Best Marine Safety Harness" the package said. What a crock of shit! That company would get a long letter upon his return. Letter? What about a law suit? A snap to win. He still had the broken safety harness trailing away from him as he slid down the swells. Proof. Come to think of it, he had thought that splice to the clip was kind of Mickey Mouse. If you're going to make a safety harness, the goddamn thing ought to work. "Don't say "Goddamn!" he shouted into the sky.

He spoke aloud, speaking upwards from the trough. "Didn't mean it, just an expression, that's all. Tell you what, if you get me out of this, I'll never use that again. I just used it as an expression. I was planning to start going to church, anyway, you know. Out on the ocean you can't go, of course. But I was going to start going as soon as I got ashore. You know, I always went to church in my head, just didn't go to the actual church. Figured that was OK. I hope, God, that that's straightened out. By the way, I'll get Brad and Hollis straightened out for you too. They're good sailors and I hope you let them be the ones that find me, because then I can tell them about you, and they'll believe me because they'll know what I went through."

The daylight went fast, and with nightfall came another depression. The darkness was like a thick black net descending over his hopeful attitude. It took away all the remaining reality he had; it took away his waves, his sky, and his horizon. And, to his weakened mind, darkness was too powerful an adversary to handle. He could no longer cope realistically with what it was. His mind was now primitive, and he reacted to the darkness the way a caveman would react to a fierce thunder and lightening storm.

In the surrounding darkness of both water and sky, he felt the petty meaning of his existence, and he felt for the first time his infinitesimal chances of survival. He wasn't being protected by the trough, and he was being prolonged and tortured and agonize and played with. The trough was now somewhere he should not be. Ever. The trough as a bad spot, a grip from down below, a whirlpool, a place where the waves, now unseen in the darkness, could overwhelm him and then suffocate him, and ultimately flood and crush his weak body until he became a pale, bloated, water-filled corpse. Never the trough.

And he panicked once again. For an hour and a half he screamed and flailed his way toward the top of each wave. He swam harder and stronger than could be imagined. The skin of the underside of his arms rubbed and chafed and eventually wore off as it rubbed the hard-stitched seam of the underarm of his heavy oilskin jacket. He swam determinedly up the top of each rolling sea, piercing the foamy crest. The sea would roll on, leaving him back in the trough. Again, he'd swim up a wave, never knowing or looking when he reached the top, but only swimming, blindly. It was his third panic. He would have covered five miles had the sea been willing to let him.

At the end of his strength, he slept once again, resting his head on the buoyant head support of the back of his lifejacket. He was much weaker and at first lacked the will or strength to keep his mouth closed. He'd doze, then suddenly be jarred awake, invaded, violated, the sea a madman torturing him with a torrent of sea water. He'd choke and gasp and try frantically to climb out of the trough. Water rushed from his mouth, nose, ears and bulging red eyes. He began to hallucinate; the waves around him became a pack of wolves, hungry and bold at times, then retreating from his sudden bursts of life.

Morning came slowly to his mind, and with it another chance to be seen. He was tired, and thought he should start taking his time looking for Hank and Brad and Hollis. Otherwise, he'd use up all his remaining strength and wouldn't be able to get to the top of the waves at all. He decided it would be wise to limit his scouting missions. He figured that every half hour would be enough. Then a terrible thought came to him: what if his whistle was broken, what if the cork ball had swollen up or disintegrated?

Quickly he reached for the whistle around his neck and put it in his mouth and blew it. Wonderful. It was as loud as ever. He grabbed it with his right hand to inspect it. It was then that he noticed his hand. It was absolutely white and shriveled and the skin seemed to be a pile of white patchwork slices glued poorly around the bone. To his shaky weather-beaten mind crept the thought that he could rot right out of his lifejacket. He saw pieces of his white flesh trailing behind him, like a snake shedding its skin. He pictured the skin from his face hanging limp, in long aged sags, and slowly, with the swish of each wave over his head, pulling his face off of his skull. All this time he stared at his decomposing hands and saw a living ghost. His will to live was drained from him, and he merely floated, his arms limp and his eyes glassy, focusing on nothing.

It was noon. The sun was clear and bright overhead. Blue sky could be seen in patches behind thick white clouds. The wind was gone, but a large swell remained from the storm. The waves were well rounded and smooth at the top. There was no more chaos from nature, at least at 36 degrees North/65 degrees West, which was approximately where he was. The sea seemed to stretch languidly off in all directions. Bermuda lay 320 miles to the south; Newport, Rhode Island, was just under 300 miles to the north. The sea undulated like a spider web in a faint breeze, and he bobbed in its grip like a tiny insect, hopelessly tangled and devoid of strength.

But he was still conscious, and he was holding the whistle again, staring hard at the silver plated object. In his mind he was back with his young wife at the seafood restaurant in the wharf in Newport. She'd said that the chances of his needing the whistle were greater than hers, and besides, she could always get another one.

"If you fall into the water you can blow it and your crew can come and get you," she'd said.

He remembered her brown eyes getting serious while saying this and he remembered putting his arm around her and saying in his baby talk voice, as he held up his tiny whistle, "This will save me, yes siree!" And he remembered she'd started to cry at the dock the last morning and he'd played tough and said "Ah, the trip will be no sweat."

Now he held his hands to his face, trying to block out both his past thoughts and present environment. The degenerated tissue of his hands against his beard-stubbled, sunburned face was too cruel a feeling, and he let his hands fall.

Images floated in where his strength ebbed out. There were thin white steeples penciled into clear blue sky, and the air was new and crisp and cold to the point that it stung his throat and lungs slightly. His hickory cross–country skis were holding their wax well, and he moved steadily through the snow, forming the tracks in which the others followed. They were far behind him, and he stopped to wait.

The silence of the Maine woods lightly teased him as he listened for the laughing voices and swishing skis of his friends. He took the wine skin from his shoulder and squirted an arc of red into his mouth. The wine was cold to his mouth and warming to his stomach. Over his shoulder, he saw the rest of them coming happily, swiftly, along the trail. His wife reached him first, gave him a kiss on the cheek, and took some wine. She was excited about the eagle she'd seen; it had soared so close and wasn't it just so beautiful here that you could stay forever, she'd said.

Big flakes fell outside the leaded glass windows of the lodge, and the owner filled them all with hot brandy and told them stories of skiers getting lost and wandering through the night in thirty-below-zero temperatures, never daring to stop moving for fear of freezing to death. Their tracks had always remained and each time, thanks to his snowmobile, he'd found them alive but scared and exhausted the next morning.

A long swell lifted him slightly and carried him west, toward the setting sun and the end of his third day. He thought about Hank whom he'd met the summer he'd met his wife, and he thought about how pale the sea and weather had made his face. He dreamed of Hank as a ghost, floating up and out of the cockpit, his yellow-hooded slicker hanging limp over a body reduced to bones and shredded dangling skin. The face that once held a full smile was now nothing but a sharp set of cheekbones and two bottomless sockets for eyes. Hank was floating up, looking for him across a great sea. He'd need help, so he blew on his silver whistle, and the sharp sound rose and curved like smoke from a chimney into the sky toward the hooded figure who floated above.

The air was calm and clear, and the sea at 36 degrees North/65 degrees West had taken on a relaxed, somehow satisfied appearance. There were no ships or planes or harsh winds to irritate. The normally chaotic Gulf Stream had turned still, as if to digest the turbulence of the last few days. Only a feeble whistle interrupted the silence and peace, and a small bobbing dot moved west with the swell toward a distant horizon.

V

OLD AGE

THE MAGICAL MYSTERY CRUISE

In nineteen hundred and thirty nine, with little fanfare or even notice by the outside world, a small cruising boat was built in a Connecticut wooden-leg factory by a man named Christ. Despite its inauspicious beginning, the boat entered the water as a beautiful sailing cutter named *Phyllis,* a vessel so pretty and able that, even now, when I look at her picture, I smile.

My grandfather had the boat built to the plans of William Atkin, a well-known marine architect. Grandfather loved her and took Grandma for a sail or two. He picked the wrong weather. Clearly she was not happy with the business of boating. " It's me or the boat. Take your pick," she said firmly after stepping ashore.

Now, good cutters are hard to come by, but finally common sense prevailed and *Phyllis* was given to grandfather's number one son, my Uncle Peter. After a sail or two, Peter's wife expressed the same sentiment her mother in law had. Again, common sense prevailed, and for the sum of $1, Uncle Peter reluctantly sold *Phyllis* to his little brother, who ultimately became my father. Unfortunately for me, the pass-down ritual did not continue. But more on that later.

My father's future wife thought it would be just fine for him to split his life between his two favorite ladies, and in 1941 my future mother, father and *Phyllis* left on their honeymoon together.

The honeymoon lasted a long time. They cruised together on *Phyllis* for nearly 40 years, through calms and storms, and through three teenage sons. They spent many summers exploring the Maine coast, and *Phyllis* became a well-known and admired sight in many a harbor.

My mother launched two sons (my two brothers) into the world in the 1940s. In 1950 I arrived as a surprise third. I came aboard *Phyllis* as a one month old that September. I'm told my basket and I were wedged under the deck beams on the forward cabin's starboard bunk. I ended up sleeping on that bunk as a baby boy, teenager and adult. As a child I remember awakening to see the naked construction of massive oak beams holding up the fir planks of the deck above me. I remember smelling the aged wood and staring at the furrows and cracks that seemed to deepen each year like the wrinkles and veins on my grandfather's face. As a child I never realized that there was a time when the planks and beams were new, uncracked and untested — a time when the structure around me was green, unchecked wood, filled with the saps and resins of youth.

They were happy years as we all grew older, a close family held even closer by a common interest in an old wooden cutter. *Phyllis* brought us together when we needed to be and took us away from one another when we became too close. My brothers and I played out our childhood fantasies on her. We divulged our adolescent secrets within her. We shared our profound young-adult thoughts and ideas about the world around her. Each summer my parents escaped their three teenage boys aboard her. And, the night it all ended, I got engaged on her.

It was a hot August evening in 1980 when the sky darkened, eclipsing what began as an interesting sunset. The air became thick and still. The whole family sat in the cockpit at our mooring in Marblehead Harbor. We'd just finished dinner. I was holding my future bride's hand, planning the best time to announce our engagement, when I noticed the rain and wind heading for us from across the harbor. We all hurried down below. The rains came, and we continued our party in the coziness of *Phyllis's* cabin, settling back on the old soft bunks or leaning against ancient mahogany bulkheads as the rain pounded the overhead and the wind heeled *Phyllis* slightly at her moorings. I don't know what brought it up, but it was then, in the midst of the storm, that my father announced he was selling *Phyllis*. My brothers and I sat in shocked silence as we listened to his plans for another, newer, easier to handle boat. The rain ran its course and I waved my two brothers up to the cockpit. "Look, we can't have this," I said. "He can't sell *Phyllis* out of the family." They both nodded in agreement.

"Then we'll just have to buy her ourselves," my brother Chris said. We nodded in agreement and went below.

I crossed my arms and looked toward my mom and dad, who sat together on the port berth, their faces aglow and seemingly ageless under the soft light of the kerosene lantern.

"Dad, we'll buy the boat," I announced with assurance.

"No you won't" he said with authority. Then he paused, gathering his thoughts. "Look, boys," he continued, "she's too old. You don't know what I know about her. She's tired. Worn out in too many places — so many places that you won't find enjoyment in owning her. Only burden." He looked at us intently for the longest time. "You need to know when to let go, "he said finally. Every era comes to an end. She's given us 40 wonderful years, and now she's done. It's time to move on. For all of us."

And damned if he didn't sell her right out from under us.

That was in 1980. For several years we were upset. But that went away when we learned that one of *Phyllis's* new owners has to replace just about every piece of her except the kerosene lantern. A subsequent owner had even worse trouble; she sank on him, we'd heard. Right to the bottom.

It seemed that Dad had been right. Ten years passed. *Phyllis* was long gone from our sight, but indelible in our minds. My parents bought a fiberglass trawler-like powerboat and proceeded to live aboard and cruise over 30,000 miles on it. Those were also good years. Then my dad had a couple of strokes, from which he recovered. But his health prompted the sale of the trawler. My parents were entering the "twilight years," and my father purchased an easier-to-handle 20-foot powerboat named *Coda*, a musical term meaning "final passage."

But it was not the final passage. It was several months before my parents' 50th anniversary, a raw spring afternoon that caused the few crocuses in the yard to wither under a thin veil of ice. The family was gathered in the family room, talking of summer plans.

"We are not sure we want to go the usual tent or VFW hall route for our anniversary," my mother said. "It just doesn't seem like us. And, besides, we'd rather be with just you kids and your wives than make a big hullabaloo with what's left of our old friends."

"What are you getting at?' I asked. "Well, 50 years ago, we spent our honeymoon on Phyllis... sailing. I think that's how we should spend our golden anniversary... sailing," my dad said. A twinkle came to his eyes.

"Let's pull out all the stops," he continued. "Charter the biggest darn sailboat you can get without a captain. The eight of us — your mother and me, and you three boys and your wives — will spend our 50th wedding anniversary cruising where we've always loved to cruise, the Maine coast. And we'll do it in style."

So in July we set sail from Camden, Maine aboard a 54-foot Alden ketch and headed east along the coast of Maine. My dad was thrilled to be sailing again — and even more thrilled to be playing with the navigation gadgets he found below deck. He looked in amazement at all the electronic wizardry: Loran, GPS, weatherfax, cellular telephone, VHF, single sideband, radar depth, speed and wind-direction gauges.

" Fifty years ago aboard *Phyllis*, " he said, "all we had was a $19 compass, a chart, a megaphone, some old Coke cans and a pencil." He paused, leaning forward to look closer at the weatherfax machine. "Did all right, too" he said, nodding his head.

"Coke cans and a megaphone?" my wife Mary Kay asked.

"We'd throw the Coke cans off the bow and time them till they reached the stern. Good way to determine boat speed," he replied. "Also, we'd stop and throw them abeam to gauge current."

"And the megaphone?"

"Oh, yes, that old red cardboard megaphone." His fingers tapped the fancy color radar screen above him. "That megaphone was my radar. I'd use it to bounce my voice off the land in the fog to find and gauge distance from obstructions."

"And that worked?" Mary Kay asked.

"Made it this far. On *Phyllis* we worked together. Sometimes we could just sense things."

We sailed from Camden to Pulpit Harbor across the bay and anchored for the night. The anniversary was three days away and we began planning the best harbor in which to have the great celebration. It brought back a flood of memories when, down in the cherry wood-finished cabin, we poured over charts detailing the harbors to which we'd all cruised aboard *Phyllis* over the years.

"Let's just see where the wind blows," my dad said finally. So we continued on east, sailing in harmony with each other and the nearly perfect July weather. On the day before the anniversary we sailed through Fox Island Thoroughfare between the islands of Vinalhaven and North Haven and headed a few miles out to sea on our way to Mount Desert Island. It was calm and we were under power. I was alone near the wheel. My dad was down below amid his array of electronic navigation equipment. The others were reading or snoozing. The ocean appeared empty; the big Alden was on auto-pilot. I casually scanned the empty hazy horizon. A speck appeared in the distance and grew larger until I could see the faintest outline of a mast and hull. It appeared to be crossing our path, perhaps a mile off. There was no particular reason for me to fixate on it. It was just another boat on a wide, wide ocean. Yet, something drew me to the binoculars. I put them to my eyes and focused on a hull that took me a millisecond to recognize.

There, as if sailing out of the twilight zone, was *Phyllis*. "Everybody? You're not going to believe this!" I yelled. " It's *Phyllis*! Honest to God. Honest to God. It's *Phyllis*." Seven more Ropers gathered on the Alden's starboard side, straining to see if this was for real. As *Phyllis* drew closer, I noticed an attractive young woman at the helm. Due to all the attention from us, she was getting anxious, self-conscious, or both. She leaned her head down *Phyllis's* companionway. A male figure popped up. The two boats were not 100 feet apart: an ancient 28-foot wood cutter and an $850,000 54-foot modern custom ketch. For what seemed eternity no one spoke. Then my father turned to me and said with a confident smirk "You planned this, didn't you?" I told him I was as surprised as he was.

Then in unplanned unison, we all shouted: "We're the Ropers, and we used to own your boat."

What happened next was the ultimate gam at sea. My family — with the exception of this writer, who felt somewhat obliged to mind our $800,000 rental — ferried over to *Phyllis* in the dinghy. It didn't take long to realize that Walter, Phyllis's new owner, was as loving an owner as my dad had been. He couldn't wait to ask my father a million and one questions about the boat's past, and about a myriad of things on board that had him perplexed.

"I can't believe I'm finally meeting you Ropers," Walter said with great enthusiasm. "*Phyllis* and the Ropers seem to be known up and down the Maine coast. It seems that everywhere I go someone comes alongside and has a story about old *Phyllis*." And on it went. If the breeze hadn't come up I think we'd all still be out there, gamming at sea.

We sailed on, leaving two new friends and plans to meet again. It was becoming a magical anniversary cruise. As we sailed east around Mount Desert Island, my dad suggested we stop in the lovely little harbor of Sorrento for the actual celebration. Later that afternoon, we picked up a guest mooring in tiny Sorrento Harbor that gave us a clear view of beautiful Cadillac Mountain across the bay on Mount Desert. With the exception of one other cruising boat, we were alone in Sorrento that night. My two brothers and our wives began preparation for the big event celebrating a half-century of marriage. Anniversary banners went up in the main salon. Scripts for skits were rehearsed. Doggerel poems were practiced. Dinner was set to simmer.

The evening grew still. At around 7 p.m., I noticed that my dad had departed in the dinghy. He had motored over to our neighbor on the other cruising boat. The air was so still that I could just make out his conversation. "It's the second biggest event of our lives," I heard him say to our Canadian yachtsmen neighbors, as he drifted alongside their sloop. " So I want to apologize in advance for any noise we might make that could harm the tranquility of this beautiful spot." It was just like him to do that. The Canadians smiled and told him not to worry. They were used to parties. And "congratulations," they said.

The party was a great success. My parents put on wigs and corsages and re-enacted their wedding of 50 years ago to the day. I remember, when the party was in full swing, I'd looked across the salon table and seen the joy reflected in my parents' eyes as they relived 50 years of memories. It was the consummate family celebration. My brothers and I re-enacted the more memorable events of our upbringing. Many were stories and skits recounting special days and nights aboard *Phyllis*. Stories of childhood fantasies. Stories of adolescent secrets. And stories of special moments as young adults — moments such as the one when, all gathered together down below deck on a stormy August night in 1980, my brothers and I had tried to keep *Phyllis* in the family.

Well, not to worry, I remember thinking. She isn't so far away after all.

Isn't Life Full of Small Surprises: Ship's Log Entries

0300 hours Dix Island

From the outside, I'm sure all appears calm, even blissful. *Elsa* is anchored in the moonlight in a quiet spot between Dix and High Islands off Muscle Ridge Channel, gateway to Maine's Penobscot Bay. The old sloop swings gently and silently under a sky of stars, seemingly transfixed by the beam of the full moon.

But below decks, there's no such serenity. Down here, jarring, cadence-challenged sounds surround me. From the bow, demonized teen-age music oozes from under the door, behind which my 15-year-old daughter, Alli, has staked her claim on the forward cabin.

Across from me in the main cabin, competing with the racket in the bow, my 85-year-old father's random throaty snores rattle the night like a mufflerless Maine pick-up truck accelerating on a bumpy dirt road.

I look over at Dad, blissful under his wool blanket. The moon, shining through the big center hatch, illuminates him in an ethereal sort of way. His hands are folded together on his stomach. I can just make out his two hearing aids, which he calls his "other ears," sitting together like two white chocolate drops on the chart table by his head. Sleeping without his other ears leaves him stone deaf, untouched by the sounds of his own snores.

Dad loves nothing better than this – sleeping aboard a boat in Maine. I could love this too if only given the chance. So I wait for the snores to stop. I stare at the stars through the hatch, thinking that, like Alli's music, his snoring has volume. If only it had some rhythm. I waited anxiously between snores, knowing that at age 85 each one could be his last. Perhaps, though, he'll just stop snoring and sleep silently.

But based on the previous seven days of cruising with this unusual and beloved crew of two, I knew what was coming: soon Dad would kick his blanket off of his feet, his toes would get cold and he'd awaken. The snoring would stop. For a few blissful moments, short of a bit of rustling as he felt around with his feet for the blanket, it would be quiet in the main cabin. I would finally fall asleep. Then I'd awake again to his loud voice (due to no hearing aides) inquiring to no one in particular as to the whereabouts of his blanket.

Next, since he was fully awake, he'd realize it was a good time to go pee, so he'd head unsteadily up the companionway steps to pee over the side. Eyes wide open now, I'd wait, hoping for only the sounds of a trickle, not a big splash. (At these moments the statistic that 78% of all drowned men are found with their flies open comes to mind).

Sometimes, after the trickle, there would be no sound at all. That's when I'd sit up in my bunk, wondering if I'd actually fallen asleep for a moment and missed the splash, and now maybe Dad was floundering in the cold Maine water. Actually, this was the period of time when Dad, now wide awake himself and sitting on the cabin roof, would be taking five or ten minutes on deck to quietly enjoy the stars.

And so it went until one night in Blue Hill Harbor I masterminded a grand plan. At the part of the above-described cycle where Dad loses his blanket off his feet, I would break it by quickly getting up, grabbing the blanket off the cabin floor, and tucking it around him before he awakened. Later, when that moment came, I sprang into action, found the blanket, tucked it around his feet, and, for good measure, tucked it under his chin. When I loomed over Dad in the darkness, I noticed his eyes were wide open staring.

I thought he was dead. Until he spoke.

"I was just thinking, "he said. "do you know that it's been 80 years since someone tucked me in? My mother used to do that. I still remember. Now you, my 50 -year old son, tucking me in. Think of that! Isn't life full of small surprise pleasures?"

2000 hours, Wreck Island, Merchants Row

Anchored amidst numerous Corinthian Yacht Club boats on their annual cruise. Dad called his girlfriend, using my cell phone. Ashore to partake in a superb clambake. Alli stayed aboard. Fog descended. Upon return to *Elsa*, I was surprised to find four sets of sneakers lined up on deck. Then I found Alli and three teenaged boys and girls below watching a DVD movie (*American Pie*). Where these three teenagers came from and how she knew them I had no idea. Made me think of gulls — there can be absolutely none in sight, but throw a piece of bread in the water, and they instantly appear from somewhere.

2000 hours. Full moon off Snow Island, Quahog Bay

Dad called his girlfriend, using my cell phone. Told her again how he missed her, how soundly he's been sleeping, and how lovely it is to be back cruising in Maine.

2200 hours.

Sat in the cockpit with Alli, both of us tucked under a fleece blanket, taking turns looking at the full moon through binoculars. The moon prompted a discussion about tides and their cycles.

"How many times does the tide come in and out, Daddy?"

"Four times in 24 hours; twice in and twice out."

"So the tide spends six hours just coming in? What does it do when it gets there?"

"Well, Alli, it goes out again."

"Well, why?" (Good question).

"Good question," I answer. (Back when I smoked a pipe, this would be when I could buy time to think of an answer while fiddling around with lighting it.)

"It seems really random," she says.

"Honey, it's anything but random."

"Well, dumb then. You know, a waste. I mean, you'd think it would stick around for awhile and *do* something after all that effort to come in."

Good point.

1400 hours, Damariscove Island

Ashore on lovely Damariscove with Dad, Alli and cruising friends Bryan and Elizabeth. Getting an 85 year old into a 7-1/2 foot dinghy from a fairly high deck is a bit of a trick, requiring a step-by-step process involving both Alli and me. We'd finally figured out the procedure, but from port to port, we often forgot the details. Fortunately, Dad records everything into the mini key chain recorder he keeps in his pocket at all times. In fact, Dad has always recorded everything. He's the only person I know who actually took notes *while* he was having a TIA, a mild transient stroke which may affect speech in areas of diction and syntax. During Dad's first TIA he said to me in the ambulance, "Worry don't Dave...only it's a slight stork I'm having." He became so frustrated and fascinated by his jumbled speech (but clear brain) that he kept a log of his thoughts at the emergency room during the stroke, to see if the written words matched his thoughts. They didn't. That log is interesting reading, believe me.

Anyway, so now he has this very low-tech (Dad thinks it's cutting edge) recording device. The only problem is that it only holds one message and then overstrikes with the next piece of data recorded.

So, upon getting into the dinghy in Damariscove, he recorded: "Sit down first, then move legs over side, then grab Alli's arm..." OK, but when he played it back at the end of the day's shore activities and his thoughts, his message had been eclipsed by a new one, delivered in one big breath: "Dave says I use too much fresh water on board; Dave says I should remember to close ice box lid right away to keep cool air in; met guy ashore named Tony Lee; I went to Taft School with his father. Small world. We need toilet paper; oh hell, just remembered this has now erased how to get into dinghy from big boat; remember to record it again when we figure it out again. Over and out."

2000 hours, same place

Dad called his girlfriend, using my cell.

Blue Hill Bay to Merchants Row, fog

GPS proved its worth today; relieved stress of navigating. Dad did quite a bit of steering. He told Alli about the "olden days" before fancy satellite navigation systems. Spoke of potato navigation, which earned him a perplexed look from his granddaughter. Grampy went on telling her about how he and her grandmother got lost in the old Atkin cutter *Phyllis* off of nearby Long Island in Blue Hill Bay. "Every direction we went, every way we tacked, we came upon land," he told her. It was very odd, like we were trapped in a box. Seemed as if we'd run a true course. Couldn't understand it. Used Coke bottles, the stopwatch; even got out the old cardboard megaphone. Nothing worked."

Alli gave me a bemused, eye-rolling, "he's really lost it" kind of look. But I shook my head. "Go ahead, Dad, explain it to her."

"What you say?"

"I SAID, GO AHEAD AND EXPLAIN IT TO HER."

"Explain what?"

"ABOUT POTATOES, COKE BOTTLES, STOP WATCHES AND OLD CARDBOARD MEGAPHONES."

"Oh, sure Dave." He grinned at me; he has fun frustrating me about his deafness. "All you need to do is ask, you know. No need to raise your voice. Dad raised himself up on his tiptoes to check for lobster pots, then he turned to Alli and smiled. "You see, Alli, we didn't have any instruments to gauge speed or drift, so we'd measure with the stopwatch the time a Coke bottle took to get from bow to stern and then do the math to figure our sped. I bet you learned that formula in school: distance equals rate times time. We'd used that old megaphone to bounce our voice off any land that might be there and gauge its distance. Worked pretty darned well. Got so you became kind of like a human radar."

Alli pushed the stop button on her Discman and looked up at him. A 70-year gap in their ages, and he actually had her attention. "Well what about the potatoes?" she asked.

" Only used them for the REAL thick fog navigation, my dear."

"You ate potatoes in real thick fog?"

"Nope, we threw them, then listened for the splash. If we didn't hear the splash, we knew land was *pretty darned* close!"

1830 hours, anchored in Billings Cove. Fog lifted

Dad called his girlfriend, using my cell phone.

1900 hours, homeport, Marblehead, MA. Final log excerpts

BEST CREW I EVER HAD. Need Sleep.

And remember to tell Dad that the cell phone bill comes to $346, including roaming changes, for his calls to his girlfriend.

BOUND TO BOATS AND LIFE

He broke his right hip when he was 87. He was lifting the battery out of *Coda*, his last and final boat, which was tied to the dock at the end of a pier. He slipped and fell, refusing to let go of the battery. No one was around. So he dragged himself up the gangway and to his car, pulled his cell phone out of the glove compartment, and called an ambulance.

When I heard him relate this story to me that night, especially the part of not letting go of the battery, it brought me back to one late summer day in 1960 when Dad and I were walking down the Hingham Yacht Club float toward the little boat we'd built together. We passed a boy about my age struggling to carry his small outboard toward his own skiff. He slipped and fell off the float. In an instant, he was gone. It was low tide, and there was only about four feet of water where he fell. Still, he went under and didn't come up. Dad got down on his knees and reached under water, felt around, finally grabbed one of his arms, and started to pull him up. "Need help," he said, "he won't come up." But just then the small boy shot to the surface and Dad pulled him onto the float. He blinked at us, coughing, while water cascaded off of his soaking clothes. "You were stuck there underwater somehow," my Dad said finally. "Not stuck," the little boy said, "I was hanging on and I didn't want to let go." He peered down into the muddy water, a devastated look on his shivering face. "My outboard," he said, "I was hanging onto my outboard down there on the bottom, but when you pulled me up it made me let go. Now it's gone." It was, no doubt, one of the boy's first lessons in how suddenly things can change for the worse.

Dad broke his other hip six years later at age 93. He was headed to his den, missed the step, and landed on the floor under the half model of the boat he spent his honeymoon on 68 years ago. This half model of *Phyllis*, the old family cruising cutter, hangs on the wall next to a framed blueprint of her line drawings. Around both of these are many pictures taken during *Phyllis'* best days...days when the old sailor and his boat were young, when *Phyllis'* youth kept the planks and ribs resilient to the turbulent and rolling seas. He may have suspected at the time that his left hip was broken, but he didn't call anyone. Not wanting to be a burden, he lay there under the half model, then finally decided to pull himself up, broken hip and all, work his way upstairs, find some bandages for the cut on his arm that came from the fall, and go to bed.

"I'm done," Dad told me he'd said aloud in the empty house that night. "Call Dr. Kevorkian. Get the angels ready, I've had enough and I'm headed up." He wasn't.

I'm writing this now at my dad's house, and thinking of how I and others have to cope. We have little training in coping, yet something seems to be built in. Not long ago I reconnected with a middle-aged friend of mine who had lost his lovely wife to cancer. "I was facing the devastation of both my life and hers, and I seemed to have no coping mechanisms," he told me. Then he tilted his head and looked lost in thought and a little puzzled. "So I began to build a strip-planked canoe. I don't know why I knew to turn that way; I just did. It kept me sane and focused on something at a time when the ground was leaving my feet."

The family home is empty now while Dad is in rehab. There's not a sound except for the grandfather clock that he built years ago; its pendulum squeaks a bit while it swings through its arc, but the old clock still goes on, though it can't keep time. Behind my chair in the big bay window are two Plexiglas cases. Each one contains a boat model; one of the *Phyllis* and the other the *Eastward*, the trawler my parents covered 35,000 miles in after Dad retired. But what's important to me now is why the models came to be. I think back more than a decade ago when my mom was bedridden for three years after a stroke. Dad was her caregiver. It was a lot to undertake for an 83 year old, but he never complained. Instead, as a relief from caring for Mom, he began to build these models of *Phyllis* and *Eastward*. He started from scratch with a stack of soft pine boards he'd glued together. From there he hollowed out, carved and faired the hulls, built all the rigging, and made fully detailed cabin interiors with miniature fixtures to match the real boats, right down to a tiny needlepoint pillow that read "Screw the Golden Years". On the cabin top of each, he substituted clear plastic, so the viewer could look down into the two-foot long cabins at all the details. Just before he sealed off the cabin top on the *Eastward* with its skylight, he placed a thimble-sized silver urn on the port bunk. "Put a few of my ashes in that someday, OK?" he said to me.

I wander into the attached garage. The nutshell pram I built years ago is stored there. It needs attention; the plywood transom has delaminated and the whole boat cries for fresh paint. The plan years ago had been to build it with my two kids, the way Dad and I had built my skiff when I was little. My kids, now grown, hadn't participated much, though. They'd had busy lives as budding teenagers. So I built it alone, once in awhile showing them my progress and attracting a vague or token interest. But I knew, deep down, it set in. I knew the seeds were planted. Someday, when amidst their own trials of life and loss, my hope is that something in them, such as the idea of building a boat, will allow them to come up with an alternative to despair.

In the garage I spot an old boat cushion on the floor and a sanding block nearby.

I kneel down on the cushion and begin to sand the delaminated transom in readiness for yet another season. Somehow, it just seems like the right thing to do.

DREAMS OF AGING SAILORS

On December 15, 2009, Kenneth Ketchum, age 80, decided to sail alone to Mexico from Houston on his Downeast 32 sailboat. He had been living in his recreational vehicle, which he sold to buy the boat. One hundred fifteen miles southeast of Houston, he was plucked from his boat by the Coast Guard ten days after leaving. The next night he spent in a homeless shelter. "I tried; I was just unable to fend for myself out there," said Mr. Ketchum, a Purple Heart medal recipient from the Korean War. At age 80, it seems, he was still making valiant efforts.

When I read this story recently, I thought back 30 years to a boat delivery of a 50-foot yawl from Duluth, Minnesota to Stuart, Florida. My crew and I were locking down in a little town called Brockport in Western New York along the Erie Canal. I was leaning against the bow pulpit, handling the forward line of the big yawl while the water drained from the lock chamber. There was a small sailboat, perhaps 23 feet, just ahead of me. An old man sat on the side of the cuddy cabin and handled his two guiding lines, which hung down from the lock high above. In hand lettered script on his boat's transom were the words "Homeward Bound, Auckland".

"Where you from?" I asked.

"Auckland," came the reply.

"No, where are you *coming* from?"

"Town of Erie, Pennsylvania. Used to live there. Lived there for sixty plus years."

"Where are you headed?"

"Auckland."

"As in Auckland, New Zealand."

"That would be the one."

There was a long pause on my end of the conversation, as you might expect.

"Soooo, how are you getting there?" I asked finally.

"I'm *headed* there on this boat," he said proudly. "I don't know if I'm *getting* there."

I think he could sense my wavering about my next comment. He continued.

"You see, I'd been sitting alone on this paint-chipped, rotting porch in this rental house for I don't know how long since retirement, and all I'd been thinking about most of those days was returning to Auckland where I was raised. It's home, really. It's still where my heart is."

I cocked my head at the tiny, far-from-seaworthy sloop and its 6 horsepower outboard.

"You think you'll make it?" I said finally.

For the first time he smiled, his face lightened by a broad, knowing look. "Don't have the slightest idea," he said, adjusting one of the lock lines. "But I figure I have two choices, given my time and financial circumstances. Plan A is to sit on that crummy porch, think that I'm stuck there, and just think about Auckland until I die in that chair. Plan B is to get there or die trying to get there. You're now witnessing me on the sixth day of Plan B. And you're witnessing a happy man with a mission."

How many of us will have a Plan B? How many of us will opt for it?

John Steinbeck suffered a stroke in December, 1959. Those close to him begged him to slow down and take better care of himself, yet he felt the very opposite: "I see too many men delay their exits with a sickly slow reluctance to leave the stage. It's bad theater as well as bad living," Steinbeck wrote. In contrast, Steinbeck fitted out his truck with a camper, named the rig *Rocinante*, took his poodle Charley as crew, and prepared to cross the United States just after Labor Day in 1960. Because of that journey Steinbeck gave us *Travels with Charley* in 1962, which was published the same year he won the Nobel Prize for Literature. In his acceptance speech he spoke of man's proven capacity for greatness of heart and spirit – for gallantry in defeat and for courage.

Westin Martyr wrote his *£200 Millionaire* in 1932. He tells of the time he and his wife were anchored in a harbor of refuge along the waterways of Zeeland in the Netherlands during a westerly gale when "a little green sloop…manned solely by one elderly gentleman" sailed in, rounded up, and eased alongside. Down below in his tiny cabin that afternoon, over a cup of tea, this old man and widower regaled the author and his wife with his tales of his solo exploration through the waterways of Europe on his tiny vessel. He talked of "gentle rivers wandering through valleys of everlasting peace; of a quiet canal, lost amongst scented reeds and covered with a pink and white carpet of water lilies; of a string of tiny lakes, their blue waters ringed with the green of forest pines; of a narrow canal, built by old Romans, but navigable still, that climbs up through the clouds into the high mountains; of aqueducts spanning bottomless ravines and a view from the yacht's deck of half of Southern Germany."

And he talked of the charm of this old earth and the fun of living on it, if "only you understand the proper way to live."

"The secret?" he was asked.

"The secret," the old man replied, "seems to be, to do everything you can yourself… Take travel. Allow yourself to be carried about the world in deluxe cabins, and what do you get out of it? You get bored to death. Everything is done for you and you don't even have to think. You're carried about with the greatest care and wrapped up and fed and insulated from … from everything. But sail all day in the wet and cold, then bring up in some quiet harbor and go below and toast your feet before the galley fire and you'll realize what bliss means. But travel in a steam-heated Pullman and then put up at the Ritz…see if you find true bliss there!"

The next day the aged wanderer was off early, catching the first of the flood tide, which would carry him into the Rhine and Germany. "Good-bye, you two," he said to the author and his wife, who gazed at him with the same awe and admiration they had the night before. He surely sensed their envy. "I don't want to influence you unduly," he said as he drifted away, "but, remember: one step does it and you're out of the rut for good."

So, to all you aging boaters out there: what will *your* one step be? What will be *your* Plan B for those years?

I'll volunteer to get the ball rolling; I'll tell you mine:

If my precious wife leaves this earth before me, and my usefulness to others has dwindled, then I'm going to buy a small cabin sailboat on a trailer. I will fill her with good wine and cheeses, with my favorite books and those I never had the time to read, and with pictures and scrapbooks to relive my old memories. But I will not dwell on these too much; I will visit them carefully the way one visits relatives: I will absorb the richness but will not linger too long. I will not linger because I will be off to make new memories each day and each season. I will travel by land to a launching ramp in Key West in the winter, watch the green flash at sunset, and then depart for the Dry Tortugas. In the late spring I'll trailer my little vessel to Lake Powell in Utah, with its majestic 2000 mile shoreline and its alluring tiny ports of Rainbow Bridge, Wahweap, Hite, and Bullfrog. I'll sail into 50-mile-long remote canyons and gaze up at the sandstone cliffs that house ancient Anasazi Native American dwellings. In the summer I will sail east to Maine and Nova Scotia and re-visit the harbors I have always loved. And perhaps one year I'll take an ambitious, international overland journey to Great Slave Lake in Yellowknife in the Northwest Territory; I'll catch lake trout and watch the Northern Lights while sailing on the fifth largest lake in North America.

And ultimately, when I am done in this world, I will be in the middle, rather than the end, of one of these journeys.

THE LAST SAIL

The boat was very tired, and the thought of getting her out of the shallow Maine cove and sailing her to Massachusetts made me feel weak and jittery. The paint on the sides had lost its high gloss finish, and had bubbled, cracked and peeled in many places. The seams between the planks were prominent, loose from many years of shrinking and swelling. The starboard side of the cabin trunk had a crack along the length of it which bisected each porthole along the way. The forward porthole had been removed, and the hole was covered with a scrap piece of delaminated plywood, like a hasty patch thrown over a wounded eye. The warmth of the cockpit varnish had long since disappeared; what was left was the cold bare structure of the mahogany, now gray with age. She sat low in the water, as if ashamed that anyone should see her condition. Green, stringy sea growth clung parasitically to what remained of her worn waterline. The early summer breeze blew in through the narrow entrance of the cove, and the thick manila halyards thumped impatiently against the tall spruce mast. A gull circled overhead, gliding silently, searching. On the other side of the cove a lobster boat's engine revved in starting, and then settled down to a steady idle.

"You said you'd take me sailing," he'd said. I stood alone beside the old sloop and remembered.

In the spring my grandmother had died. Grandfather wanted to live alone and fend for himself "until I get back together with your grandmother," as he put it to me after the funeral. There was no doubt in his mind that he would join her; it was just a question of time, he'd said. I couldn't argue with that, but I told him

I had to get back to Minnesota, where I was living. I said I'd see him in the summer when I'd return for a visit. He said I'd probably not see him; he just wouldn't be around, but off with Grandmother. He smiled at me. He was such a formal man, and I knew he wouldn't think it quite proper, but I gave him a hug anyway. I couldn't accept the fact that he wouldn't be there. He was too special, too big a chunk of my life.

"I want you to have the boat," he said, his chin over my shoulder as I hugged him. "Do what you think is best for her when you return in the summer."

"I'll take you sailing when I get back," I said.

He looked at me for the longest time, but he didn't say anything. There was a wondrous expression on his face. I didn't know what was happening or what he was thinking. Slowly, I stood up. Maybe this was "passing away" and some angel had gracefully entered him and filled his face with wonder. In my short twenty one years, I'd never seen anyone die. His speech jolted me.

"Wouldn't that be something? You know, your grandmother never did like sailing, and it was always a chore for me to get away on the sloop." He chuckled. "It will probably be the same way in the hereafter, if they have sailing there. This could be my last shot at it David."

Over the next couple of months he grew weak, had a stroke, and lost sight in one eye. Too frail to care for himself, he still refused to burden my parents in any way. He went to a nursing home. He didn't like the place, so, I suppose, his mind clogged it out, and he put himself back in the past. My mother wrote that he spoke often of me and hoped he could see me; he had something to ask me. He wouldn't tell my mother what it was.

When I returned that summer, I went to see him in the nursing home. I'd never been in one before. It looked like the junior high school I taught in: long and austere, a one level brick building with a flat roof. There were few trees. In the hall I smelled disinfectant and heard nothing. I rounded the first corner. The hallway was filled with wheelchairs. The silence made my head throb. In the wheelchairs were remnants of long lives, people whose bodies continued to work through sheer force of habit. Their chairs seemed to be swallowing them while they stared blankly into the present, as if melting away into their memories. I moved along, looking for Grandfather. It was meant to be that I had to go through much of the home to find him. When I finally did find his room, I knew what he'd wanted to talk about. Sitting in the corner, he stared out the window. As I put my hand on his shoulder, he turned and looked at me. One eye looked right into me; the other, the one the stroke had taken, looked away into nowhere.

"You said you'd take me sailing," he said. "This place is the doldrums."

* * *

As I stepped aboard the old sloop, those memories faded. I noticed that she lacked the spring and buoyancy she used to have. I knew the bilge must be full of water. Reaching under the aft cockpit hatch, I felt around for the key to the cabin. It was there on the hook, probably untouched since Grandfather had put it there months ago. She had been wet stored, uncovered, in the little Maine harbor the previous winter, and Grandfather had been up only once to see her and check on things. After my grandmother died, Grandfather had, for the first time in decades, neglected his sloop. Water was above the floorboards, beginning to claim the bunks. I pumped 300 strokes on the old fashioned bronze bilge pump and then rested, sitting on the horsehair mattress on the port bunk. The exertion from the pumping made me realize the amount of work that lay ahead, and a sense of futility began to leak into my mind. Then a lobster boat passed close by, its wake slapping the old sloop's hull. She shot upward, rising to the intruder, limberly bouncing over the next wave. I smiled. My apprehension left. "We just might make it," I said, patting the inside of the hull.

Two days later she was in fair enough condition to attempt the 100-mile sail to Massachusetts. I wanted to bring her to Grandfather, so he could sail her and still be close to his doctors and the hospital. His sloop still looked neglected, with the engine way beyond hope, a rusted block of afterthought claimed by the salt air. But her rig was in order, and the sails passable. And I'd cleaned off that encroaching green waterline slime. It was enough; I wasn't sure just how much time I had to spare. We sailed. Not fast, but true, slicing to windward with a purpose. The winter's growth on her bottom and the tide fought us. And the next morning, when the southwest wind blew hard on the nose, the waves fought us. I worried for the seams, the tired ribs, and the tall spruce mast. Still, we sailed. Newer boats passed us handily. It wasn't like the old days, when she could easily show her stern to many of her challengers. Now when we were passed, we weren't noticed; we were suddenly insignificant, and that hurt the most. I cursed the shiny younger boats, trying to ignore them as they did me.

The lighthouse of the harbor near the nursing home appeared off the bow. The old compass was dead on. The sloop rounded up easily inside the breakwater. I ran forward and let go of the jib halyard, and then dropped the old Herreshoff anchor with twenty fathoms of chain attached. As I let go the main halyard, the sail hesitated, and finally I had to yank it down.

He was in the corner looking out the window just as I'd last seen him. I walked around in front of him slowly, so as not to startle him. He looked at me and sighed deeply. In fact, he sighed so hard it scared me.

"Grandfather, don't do that!"

"Don't do what?"

"Sigh so hard."

"What so hard?"

"Sigh. Sigh so hard. It scares me."

He smiled and gave me his high pitched laugh. "Oh, rubbish," he said. Pausing, he looked out the window and then looked back at me. "Look, I'll tell you when I'm going to die. Ok?"

He had sensed my embarrassment and lifted me out of it.

"You got her here safely, didn't you? I *know* you did."

"She's ready," I said with pride. "She's here. We're going sailing."

His good eye looked toward the hall. "Yes, but David, we have a problem with a Mrs. Blake, the head nurse. It seems she is adamantly against this."

"We're going," I said, adamantly.

He seemed very relieved at the determination in my voice. He smiled and tried to adjust himself in the wheelchair.

"I've been working on Mrs. Blake," he said. "I've made myself a terrible burden and told her I shan't die until I go on that last sail."

"How does she take that?"

"Well, now she blames the whole thing on you." Then he smiled deeply, a crooked smile knocked off balance by his bad eye, which couldn't follow the aim of his grin. "You'd better start right now looking for another nursing home for yourself David, because when you're ready, in five or six decades, this one will never take you. At least not if Mrs. Blake is still around. She doesn't take to people who try to stir up a little excitement around here. 'It strains the heart' as she says."

"Mrs. Blake will be six feet under by then," I said, laughing and shedding for the first time some of my hang-ups about death.

"I wouldn't be so sure," he laughed. "She seems quite determined to hang around until she sees the whole world through a quiet, sedate, and uneventful life and death."

She was at the front desk when we left. I simply said to her: "I'm taking my grandfather sailing this afternoon."

"He's in no condition for that," she replied quickly, turning her head and brushing back a long strand of hair from her eyes.

"Mrs. Blake," my grandfather interrupted, leaning forward in his wheelchair. "Then what, pray tell, am I in condition for?"

"She's not in the best condition," I said in the taxi. Grandfather sat on the far side of the seat, smiling and clutching the arm rest on the cab door. Looking around, he was very happy to be out in the world again, even in a cab.

"Oh, forget that old bag," he said.

I laughed. "No, Grandfather, I meant your sloop."

He chuckled and we rode on in silence, past the pungent salt-water marshes that surrounded the road.

"Is that forward seam leaking again?" he asked, finally.

"Yes, pretty bad underway. But it won't be a problem for short day sailing."

"Never could fix that leak," he said, shaking his head.

I paid the driver, and we both helped Grandfather out of the cab and into his wheelchair. I'd brought the sloop to a dock with a wide gangway attached, so I could more easily wheel him down to her and get him aboard. At the top of the ramp he saw her. His good eye took his boat in fully, lovingly. "My, my, David, you did get her here. You got her here. Wonderful!" On the dock, I put one arm under his legs, my other around his back, and lifted him up. It was no great strain. He was so willing, he almost floated from the wheelchair into the cockpit seat.

"We've got a day for it, haven't we?" he said, looking at the sky and then at the wind direction indicator at the top of the mast.

"Perfect. I'll do the legwork and you handle the helm," I said, going forward to raise the mainsail. I cast off the bow, stern and spring lines. Grandfather adjusted the main sheet, and we slid neatly out of the harbor while I unfurled and then hoisted the jib. We sailed southeast, down the south shore of Massachusetts. The wind blew heartily, and as a puff hit and the rail went under, I watched Grandfather unflinchingly hold his course, refusing to round up and spill a little wind. He knew the limitations of his sloop, and he pushed them to the edge. He sailed her in toward Plymouth, and I tried to imagine what it must have been like for the Pilgrims, feeling their way in here more than 300 years ago. Grandfather sailed her a little farther down the coast, past the nuclear power plant. "Used to be horses running about where that thing is now," he said. He paused and looked at the sails, making sure he was taking full advantage of the wind. "I hope all this energy crisis business works out for you," he said. "And I hope that thing doesn't blow up, or whatever happens when atoms go haywire." He tacked the sloop away from the coast, out to sea. He did the maneuvering by himself, and I watched, detached and somehow alienated, as the two of them, products from a different age, sliced to windward, away from the stark square structure that occupied the hill where the horses used to roam.

We were both aware of the weakening daylight and stretched the day out as far as we could. But I didn't want to try to make the harbor entrance after dark, and I persuaded him to come about and make for home, saying that we'd have some coffee down below decks in the cozy cabin. It was one of those things I knew he loved. He was quiet on the way in, and it seemed finally that he was satisfied with the sail. He rounded her up gracefully at the dock. I tied her off and furled the sails, while Grandfather coiled the main sheet.

The sun was beginning to recline on the horizon, and over the land behind us the sky spread to a blanket of red. I went below to heat up some water and check the level of seawater in the bilge. Grandfather sat in the cockpit, fading to an outline in the dwindling daylight. I pumped a hundred strokes while the coffee water heated. I heard him talking faintly. "My room faced north in the nursing home, and I never got much of a chance to watch the sun," he said.

I looked up from my pumping. "You should get a different room," I said.

He continued, apparently not hearing me. "Sunsets are precious things. Powerful things. One should never take a good sunset for granted."

It took some time, but I managed to get him down the companionway ladder below decks. I made him comfortable on the
port berth, and together we sipped steaming black coffee. When I
poured him more, he tapped the bunk and said, "Now *this* is a nursing home."

I changed the subject. "What do you suppose the deal is with
that leak up forward? I pumped a hundred strokes again."

He thought for awhile. "It may be a stopwater gone bad up
where the stem joins the keel, or just a hunk of caulking missing
somewhere."

"Well, this fall I'll check into both those things when I haul her
and get her fixed for good."

"You think that will be the end of it?" he asked softly.

"It couldn't be anything else," I replied, missing the point.

For the first time he looked at me as if I were a child, and not a
friend. "David, she is very old, and when you try to get at the stem,
you'll find the fastenings on the planks weak and deteriorated,
and the planks will be soft and punky around the fastenings. And
when you do get to the stem, you'll find that piece of oak tired and
maybe not able to hold new fastenings. And the stopwater between
the stem and the keel may be deteriorated, but that, by then, will
be inconsequential." He shook his head slowly. "She's old, David."

"So what do I do?" I asked.

His eyes reflected the last bit of the sun's radiance. He blinked
twice, both times so slowly I thought I'd never see his eyes again.
But they appeared, holding a look that seemed utterly tired yet
utterly satisfied.

"You can get me a blanket, so I can take a beautiful long nap on
my lovely old sloop," he said. He smiled and then slowly he closed
his eyes.

Please share your thoughts;
I'd love to hear from you.
davidroper00@gmail.com

CPSIA information can be obtained at www.ICGtesting.com
Printed in the USA
LVOW012033081212

310752LV00017B/1075/P